Can You See the Wind?

Can You See the Wind?

A Novel

BEVERLY GOLOGORSKY

Seven Stories Press
New York · Oakland · London

Seven Stories Press
140 Watts Street
New York, NY 10013
www.sevenstories.com

College professors and high school and middle school teachers
may order free examination copies of Seven Stories Press titles.
Visit https://www.sevenstories.com/pg/resources-academics
or email academics@sevenstories.com.

Library of Congress Cataloging-in-Publication Data

Names: Gologorsky, Beverly, author.
Title: Can you see the wind? : a novel / Beverly Gologorsky.
Description: New York, NY : Seven Stories Press, [2021]
Identifiers: LCCN 2021032778 (print) | LCCN 2021032779 (ebook) | ISBN
    9781644211106 (trade paperback) | ISBN 9781644211113 (ebook)
Subjects: LCGFT: Proletarian fiction. | Novels.
Classification: LCC PS3557.O447 C36 2021 (print) | LCC PS3557.O447
    (ebook) | DDC 813/.54--dc23
LC record available at https://lccn.loc.gov/2021032778
LC ebook record available at https://lccn.loc.gov/2021032779

Printed in the USA

9 8 7 6 5 4 3 2 1

For Maya, especially and always

And with deep appreciation

For
Elizabeth Strout
and
Jane Lazarre

Like a Door Opening

Sometimes it feels
like a door closing
as if we are talking
about me leaving you
forever, even if I am
saying, I am not leaving you
ever, I am saying
it feels like a door closing.

But then it feels like a door
opening—to what or where
I don't know, and I rush
for air, and if some wind
blinds me momentarily
I close my eyes,
I do not want to look
into your eyes or away from you,
so I look at the door
then over my shoulder until
as if in ordinary time
I say good-bye.

First, the door I leave half open—
then the one I close tight.
I rush into the street
for air, and though the wind
blinds me momentarily,
and I close my eyes,
I am grateful for the night.

—Jane Lazarre, from *Breaking Light*

November 1971

Josie paces the side of the church in head scarf and dark glasses. No one must recognize her. Her eyes rest on the slate tombstones slim as ancient teeth; a plastic sheet drapes a mound of freshly dug-up earth. Beneath a cloudless blue sky, black telephone wires stretch through treetops like unfinished notes.

Inside, the church is small with no cathedral ceilings or stained-glass windows, honey-colored wood everywhere. The mahogany casket an angry gash, as imposing as its inhabitant.

September 1971

The razor leaves wide naked swaths across Celia's scalp as her hair accumulates in the sink. The activity feels secret, like a prison escape. Her long beaded earrings now irrelevant, she drops them in the empty soap dish, while her eyes remain fixed on the mirror, on the image of her as a bald woman.

Hair grows back. Some losses, though, are final.

January 1967 and After

PART ONE

-I-

On the El train platform beneath a bruised sky, Josie takes in the tarred rooftops of the stunted gray buildings that make up the Bronx. This is where she was born. But being born somewhere doesn't make it forever. She reads books, though her mother regards them as dust gatherers. It used to annoy her, and maybe it still does. But protesting her mother's attitude would do no good. Perhaps it's because her mother wasn't born here and simply can't understand what's important to Josie. What's difficult, though, is growing up within a family where everyone sees her future through the tiny lens of his or her own life. It makes her want to shout no, but she's learned to abide.

She exits the subway and heads to the Peacock Cafe, her Greenwich Village weekend sanctuary where artists, poets, and political people congregate. Captured by their conversations, which are rarely whispered, she learns a great deal, especially about the Vietnam War, which is on everyone's lips.

Maisie and Nina, two NYU students, invited her to join their table several weeks ago. They, too, are actively part of the growing antipathy to the war. Their certainty about their beliefs impressed her at once. And their assumption that she shared their views pleased her.

She didn't mention that her brother Richie had signed up for the army. It's still possible that he won't pass the physical.

He has allergies, needs glasses. He used to memorize the school eye chart, because who could afford glasses? He says the army will teach him a trade, even fix his teeth, and besides, he'd be drafted anyway. She didn't want Richie to enlist, pleaded with him, but to no avail. They'll equip him to kill for no good reason. Some men have it in them. Not her brother. The war will devour him.

Finding a table for three, her eyes rest on the wraparound mural of the Amalfi Coast, near where her parents were born. The mural is old and flaking in spots, but the green-golden mountains atop the blue sea are beautiful to behold.

Maisie swings in on a gust of cold air. "Forget coffee. We're going to a meeting. Nina's already there."

She follows her friend through a maze of university hallways to a classroom with a closed door. Seated inside around a table are Nina and two men. Maisie introduces Josie to Lowell and Ben. With only a nod to her, their talk continues. With their excited voices and gesturing hands, their conversation could be mistaken for a run-through of a play without costumes.

"Did you read McNamara's spiel in the *Times* yesterday?"

"They lie without batting an eye."

"Do they think we're idiots?"

"They're murdering in our name."

"Not my country right or wrong."

"Hey, the Communists are landing at Malibu."

"They're easy to see, green scaly skin."

"They can't fight this fucking war without us."

"We have the power to make a difference."

"We'll escalate every time they do."

"They can't get away with sending more troops. Wake up, campus! Wake up, people! We'll get the message out."

"Whatever actions we take will feed into the DC march. Who in their right mind wants this obscene war? I'd rather be jailed than kill innocents."

"Don't waste time telling us what we already know," Nina says. "Talk about ideas."

Empty coffee cups line the table like soldiers.

"Spray-paint antiwar slogans. At dawn," Lowell says.

"Where?" Nina asks, impatient.

"The Midtown building that houses Honeywell offices. The bastards make cluster bombs. But we should wait until Monday when people return to work," Ben says.

Their optimism is infectious, a kind of blind faith. Their faces unchecked by negatives, success is a given. The energy, certainty, the whole scene, charges Josie's brain; only their sense of entitlement feels alien. It's as if they can have what they want by declaring it so.

"Are you with us, Josie?" Ben whispers, his bright eyes playful.

She nods.

"We'll meet back in this room at four, and bring slogans. Okay, let's split." Lowell calls it as if it's a football move.

She, Nina, and Maisie head out together. The freedom of their long gauzy skirts only adds to her desire. These are the women she wants to live with, though she hasn't told them so. But wanting and getting are miles apart.

"How about 'No more war'?" Nina suggests.

"Too general," Maisie says.

"'US out of Vietnam' is the point."

"Perfect," Maisie says.

"Two more?" Nina says.

"Painting the same slogan everywhere is powerful," Josie offers.

"Yeah," Maisie agrees. "One strong one. It's what Madison Avenue thrives on."

"Fine," Nina says. "I'm out of here. You guys heading to the café?"

"My job search begins this minute," Josie hears herself say.

"Where?" Maisie asks.

"Around here."

"Part-time gig after school?" Maisie asks.

"No, full-time. I'm moving out of my parents' place. I'll need somewhere to crash, a couch or mat, a key in my pocket. I'll chip in for the rent." Her words as eager as her wish.

"We have a pullout," Maisie says more to herself. "How long would you stay?"

"Till I find something I can afford on my own," she promises herself.

"Okay with me," Nina says. "It's eighty a month. Could you swing twenty?"

"Absolutely. Can I move in this weekend?"

"There's no room for more furniture."

"My clothing, a clock . . ."

-2-

People dash past Celia with enough purpose for one to assume they're on the way to significant destinations. Or it may simply be to escape the cold, raw wind. She, too, rushes, but it has nothing to do with weather. She's late for work.

When the alarm rang this morning, no one budged, including her. Then they were all scrambling at once to get ready.

As usual Quincy was first in the bathroom, while Miles waited slumped in a chair, his eyes open but still asleep. If she'd asked what time he went to bed, he would have been upset. He's seventeen, easily upset. Sam was the only one not waiting for the bathroom. Her husband had named the first two boys, but she had fought against the youngest becoming some musician's afterthought.

Someday she'll toss out the alarm clock and lie in bed in a gorgeous haze of unscheduled pleasure. On that day money will drop from heaven. What's money really worth, Celia? That's Paul's singsong cadence in her head, instructing her to take it easy, cool the sweat, lighten up, go slow. But her babies, who are no longer babies, need everything. By now Paul is in Ontario. One more gig in Canada, another in Albany, then home for a while. His kind of music is on the wane, though he's still on the road more than she'd like. He's also getting high more often than she'd like. No worse than a truck driver taking NoDoz, he assures her. Her husband lives on the edge by choice, a man who's been backslapped by mobsters, fooled by tricksters, slipped the occasional hundred-dollar tip by the slumming mink crowd. He offers his experiences to her lovingly, in detail. And she's a sap, has been, will be, and so what?

The three-story Bronx factory building is on Third Avenue in the shadow of the El train. Celia hurries up the three flights between narrow dark walls that reek of old fruit. As she pushes open the heavy metal door, it all looks the same as yesterday: rectangular room with two large windows, a cutting table, four rows of six sewing machines, ceiling lights, tiny lamp in each work space. She sews silk and nylon material into slips, sometimes negligees. She is one of twenty-four seamstresses paid by the finished garment. Some days she can earn twenty dollars, less if there's lace to apply.

At her workspace is a pile of cream-colored satiny pieces cut to become thigh-length slips, the kind that movie stars wear under their dresses. She considers taking one for Josie, then turning back the tally. Everyone does it.

Blowing dust off the surface, she threads the needle and switches on the machine. To keep the material from bunching up, she needs to hold each piece straight and tight with elbow and wrist as her fingers pass the seams under the fast-moving needle. Her foot pedals the treadle automatically.

"Celia, I need a favor." Artie's large hand appears near hers. "Stop a minute. A shipment of silk came in this morning. It's a one-time order. Kimonos. I need people to stay several hours longer. I want a few dozen by tonight. Say yes."

"What about my sons?"

"Call them. Use the office phone."

"My sister's coming for dinner."

"You'll be out of here by seven, not a minute later."

With his bushy dark brows, curly black hair, big round shoulders, he could pass for a caveman. Except he's too young, maybe forty, though some of the women believe he's older.

"Seven p.m., that's a long day. I get double time after four."

"What union is this?"

"Celia deluxe."

"Okay. I can spring for three hours."

"Everyone who stays will expect double!" she shouts at him as he disappears into the glass cage of his office.

When the noise of the machines subsides, she weaves her way to the back room to find her sandwich in the fridge, then sits across from Denise and Adele at the long table.

"Vi's coming in tomorrow. Artie told me."

"For bookkeeping?"

"For cooking the books."

"She's not an accountant."

"But Vi's his wife."

"Not much of one, I hear."

"Rumor, rumor."

"Maybe, but Artie's looking old for his age."

"It's good his wife controls the money," Celia says, wondering how much Paul will bring home.

"It's not all she controls."

"A woman with her hands in the till is better off than one with her hands on a prick. Remember that."

"Adele, you're too focused on sex."

"I am?"

"The whole week you're bringing up men's private parts," Denise says.

"Is that true?" Adele asks Celia.

Celia nods. Talking about nothing that matters is their route through doors usually kept locked.

"Jesus, what do you think it means?"

"Oh, you don't want us to speculate."

"Denise, leave her be. She's worried. I understand."

"But you know where Paul is when he's not at home. Adele hasn't a clue."

"How long has it been this time?" Celia asks, not wanting Paul to be part of the conversation.

"Four days. I spoke to his friends on the construction site. Either their lips are glued, or they really don't know where he is."

"It's classic. They get a whiff of forty and go nutsy. If you were rich, you could buy him a Jaguar, let him race around Montauk, get in touch with his aura of eternal youth." Denise waves her arms as if invoking some spirit.

"Why aren't you thinking hospitals or police or accident?" Celia asks.

"Adele, do you want sex morning, noon, and night? Do you have a life outside of bed? A few days holed up with young flesh, he gets it out of his system, returns, and can't do enough to please you. On the other hand, if you don't hear from him after a week, change the locks and good fucking riddance." Denise takes a bite of her sandwich.

"You're probably right."

"What do your daughters know?" Celia is curious about fathers in other people's homes.

"I don't want to sully the bastard in their eyes. I say he's working construction in Baltimore and I'm not sure when he'll return. My oldest looks at me with pity like she knows something I don't."

"Are you staying to work on the kimonos?" Celia asks.

"Would you list our choices?"

"Hi, I'm home, finally." Celia shrugs off her coat, kicks off her shoes, and joins her sister and sons on the floor where a half-eaten pizza pie is cooling on the coffee table.

"Richie got the date for his physical," Josie says.

"He can't follow orders," Quince says.

"He won't make it through basic," Celia adds, eyeing the dark cabinet where red wine waits.

"Something else too. I found a job as a hospital file clerk. I'm moving into Manhattan. Don't even think of arguing. No more will I be stuck in this borough. I want life," Josie announces.

"Life?" Celia repeats.

"*This* isn't it." Josie gestures toward the room. "I intend to have a thousand million experiences and not remain hidden in the closet of a family."

"You're in your last year of high school." A waste of words. Josie's as stubborn as their mother and twice as determined.

"School's a joke. I learn nothing. I'm bored. I can take courses anytime."

"You and Miles are college material."

"Where's it written that everyone has to go at eighteen? You could attend college now, Celia. Rules about how and when to do things, it's a setup to make us imitate our parents' lives. Not me."

"Will you make enough to pay the rent?" Miles says.

"I'm sharing an apartment with two women."

"Will I see you as often?" Miles asks.

"Your school is within walking distance of my new apartment."

"Miles needs to come home after school to take care of his brothers."

"Stop trying to hold it all in place, Celia. Everything is changing. It's in the air, a wind blowing many voices. I'm paying attention. You should too."

"Mom, it's about being young," Quince informs her.

Her sons seem mesmerized by Josie's pronouncements. She, however, finds her sister's notions irritating and adolescent.

"Listen up. I have a letter from your father." She dips into her purse for the envelope and reads.

> *To my Son-shines,*
> *Last night, when I began to play, I heard your voices, bass and treble, thick and thin, the sounds around you. Rain on car tops, gravel underfoot, wind shaking leaves, somewhere a cat mewing, the sharp beep of a horn on a quiet Sunday. Suddenly Sully heard what I was hearing and began echoing my notes. And good old Roper recorded the whole deal and named it "Urban Stew."*
> *The three of you with me.*
> *Pop*

-3-

Josie stuffs the last of her clothing into a duffel bag, then drags it to the bedroom door for Richie to pick up. He's driving her to the new apartment.

In the kitchen, crouching tigers await her: Johnny, Terry, her mother. No matter what anyone says to dissuade her, she'll stay focused on her new place and her new friends.

The narrow hall leading to the kitchen ends too soon. Her mother stands in front of the refrigerator, hair in a bun, lips ironed shut, arms folded across her chest, a big woman, more square than round, who tells everyone what to do but never why.

"Come in. Make yourself at home even if you are leaving us." Johnny pulls out a chair, which she ignores.

Richie is loitering nearby. "My bag's ready," she informs him.

"You can change your mind." Johnny's voice playful.

"Why would I do that?"

"So you don't cause Ma the same kind of grief your cousin Grace did her mother when she ran away."

"I left the address in my room, Ma, phone number too. I'm not running away." But is she?

Her mother says nothing.

"Do you realize what you're leaving?" Johnny shakes his head. "Everyone around here looks after you. You can't buy that."

"Richie, my bag please." Who clipped his tongue? He could throw a few helpful words her way.

"I hear you got a job. Where?" Terry's voice overly pleasant, but nothing fractures the tension.

"St. Vincent's Hospital." Does her mother plan to move from that spot?

"Now, that's a safe environment." Terry offers this as reassurance to the others. Josie's sister-in-law's been a member of the family since junior high school when she and Johnny began going steady. Josie has never been able to figure out if Terry married Johnny because he's handsome, which he is in a Steve McQueen way, or because she enjoys being dominated. After two years of trying to conceive, Terry won't ask him to go for a sperm test.

"What are they paying you?" Johnny asks.

"I don't inquire after your salary."

"Just looking out for your welfare."

Several cheeses, a sliced tomato, and Italian bread are on the table. Even if she were hungry, she wouldn't prolong the ordeal by a mouthful.

"Taking off this way is an insult to the family." Johnny dips a piece of bread into some oil, holds it out to her.

"No thanks."

"Your family wants to take care of you till you're married. You're not letting us do our job," he says.

"I'm not a child."

"You live apart from family, men won't treat you with respect." He pops the bread in his mouth.

She speaks directly to her mother. "Girls my age are on the go. It's a different time."

"Cousin Grace is stuck in some drug-infested den. Sorry, Ma." Johnny glances at his mother.

"You don't know that." Her cousin lived on the same street, went to her school, was in all of the same classes through tenth grade when she disappeared. Though they had shared secrets, Grace had never told her she was leaving.

"Hey, I'm a cop. I cruise the streets. You can't imagine what I see. Ma worries about what'll happen to you out there."

"Honey, let her be." Terry touches his shoulder.

He shrugs her off. "Ma believes you don't care about her anymore."

"How do you know what Ma believes?"

"Josie, don't," Terry warns.

"I'll phone you in a few days, Ma. Okay?" But her mother remains mute.

She kisses Terry's cheek, then follows Richie out into the dark hall, down five flights, and to his car parked in front of her parents' pizzeria. "Wait out here for me. I'll only be a minute."

The place is small, with only two tables. Her father, wrapped in a large white apron, is seated at one, his thin arm resting on the marbled Formica. He looks sad, worried, tired. How long can he keep up a fifteen-hour day? Still, if they sell, what'll he do? Who would he talk to? She shudders.

Tony, a neighborhood kid who works there, is punching dough near the oven, a steel monster large enough to cremate a body.

"Hi, Pa," Josie says.

He nods.

She pulls up a chair, rests her arm near his. "Ma has all the information."

He nods.

"It's a safe apartment with two women students. NYU's just a skip away. You can bring Ma down for a visit. It's only a train ride."

"We'll see."

But he won't see. They'll never visit. Manhattan is outside the parameters of their life. "Has it been slow all afternoon?"

"They come in later, after the movies."

"Ma's not speaking to me. Tell her I'm not running away. Tell her thousands of young women move out before they're married. It's the American way." But she knows her departure is already being recorded as one more event out of their control.

"She'll get used to it."

"And you?"

His warm hand comes down on hers. "You're a good girl."

With his elbow out the window, four fingers on the steering wheel, Richie careens around, cutting corners so close she expects to end up on the sidewalk.

"I hope you're more careful with a tank."

He smiles.

"Why didn't you say a word in the kitchen?"

"What's the point? You can't change them. All you can do is reassure them that you won't die."

"You sound wise, but I think you're chicken for enlisting."

"I don't mind going. I'm tired of waking up to the same boring chug of espresso machines."

"Or garlic smells."

"And cheese."

"Shalimar perfume *everywhere*."

"And pissy hallways."

"Richie, not true. Everything is kept sparkling."

"So who cares?" He stares ahead.

"Exactly. I need to make a life. Understand?"

"Perfectly."

"So why didn't you say something nasty to Johnny?"

"He wasn't razzing me."

"How can Terry stand it?"

"Terry won't bark at him in front of others. It's different at home."

"Do you know that?"

"That's how women are, right?"

She can't tell if he's teasing. "Johnny would be happy living in Italy."

"I'd rather learn about what I don't know."

"First intelligent remark I've heard today. What a trade-off, see the world and die. I'll write you often." She touches his hand on the wheel.

"Don't send me antiwar propaganda."

"Being informed doesn't end because you're a soldier."

"It's a challenge to bunk with guys who think you're a traitor."

"You could organize them."

"To go drinking, sight-seeing, that's it, Josie."

"I can't promise to suppress my feelings."

"Then think about what I need." His tone is serious.

"I will, all the time. And, Richie, you have to level with me. Don't write me a bunch of crap about how well things are going. The truth and only the truth, so help you God, Mary, and the rest of the trio."

"And what'll you do with all that truth? Come and get me?"

"I can't be helpful unless I understand what's happening to you. So, promise."

"The gory shit is yours." But he doesn't look at her.

Still clutching the key to the new apartment, she walks through the rooms. It's as she imagined: political posters covering the walls and books everywhere. In the high-ceilinged living room, an overstuffed couch, two beat-up chairs, and protected by an Indian spread, the pullout she'll sleep on. The studied carelessness of the place is comforting, something her home doesn't offer.

Afternoon sunlight streams through the tall uncurtained kitchen window. The view reveals university buildings and a glimpse of Washington Square Park. On the white-tiled counter, a can of coffee and some filters. She prepares a pot of fresh coffee for her friends. As she listens to the drip, drip of the liquid, the strangeness of the newness is already fading.

-4-

The first glimmers of daylight appear in the sky, though the moon remains visible. Josie has never been outdoors this early, certainly not in Midtown Manhattan. Free of traffic, Sixth Avenue is a wide naked corridor between skyscrapers.

Last night, her second in the apartment, both of her friends couldn't settle.

Maisie went to bed early; so did Nina after her father called to wish them luck. No one in Josie's family would wish her luck unless she followed the chosen path: high school diploma, secretarial job, nice young man, marriage, and don't wait long to get pregnant. Her trajectory is already different. Once she asked her father, "Are you happy?" He said, "Who is happy?"

A few streets from where she's to meet Ben, a man in a long shabby coat steps out of a doorway and walks close behind her. She isn't sure how to respond. What if he follows her to the action? What if he's an undercover cop? What if she's arrested for defacing property? It would cause a family scandal. They wouldn't have to know. Her friends would bail her out. Their lawyers would appear at the arraignment. The whole episode would be an experience, which is what it's about.

"What do you want?" she demands, turning around, her tone sharp.

Bewilderment crosses the man's face. He stretches out a hand

and begins to babble at the rate of a thousand words a second. What's the matter with him?

"Go away," she says.

He looks at her curiously, round eyes worried.

Perhaps he's a beggar? She holds out a nickel. He shakes his head vigorously and points ahead as if warning her about something only he sees.

Her eyes follow the direction of his finger. "Nothing there," she mumbles.

He nods sagely as if to say, It's coming.

She decides he's a prophet sent to test her street smarts. She's on her own now, isn't she? "Okay," she agrees, and continues walking.

He follows a few feet behind.

Ben waits at the appointed spot near the building. "Who's your friend?"

She turns and waves good-bye to the man. He shuffles off with a backward glance.

"Who is he?"

"My guardian angel."

"Everyone needs one." Ben hands her a can of red spray paint, which makes the action real. She stuffs it in her jacket pocket and again remembers last night. She sat alone with the TV news, awful scenes from the war filling the screen as newsmen described a firefight in hushed tones, and the camera panned over mangled bodies awaiting helicopter pickup. The war took hold of her in a way that it hadn't before: a flesh-and-blood event occurring each second of every day rather than anyone's idea of it. She wants to be able to do something, anything, to call attention to the carnage.

The building that houses the Honeywell offices is massive, with entry through three rotating doors. Nina and Lowell were there earlier and, in very tall bright red letters, had spray-painted the slogan above the main entrance. Seeing it, a jolt of adrenaline rips through her. With heart racing, she aims the can at the facade and paints the antiwar slogan again and again as fast as she can until the moon disappears into the white sky.

Josie warms her fingers around a mug of coffee. She has only a few minutes to spare before having to leave for work. They've all met back at the apartment to assess the action.

"A toast to success," Ben says.

"People will be walking past our slogans right now," Maisie adds. "I'd love to see some exec's face as he enters the building."

"It was very well thought out," Nina says. "What's wrong, Josie? You look as if you don't agree."

Concerned that she hasn't yet earned the right to be critical, she hesitates. But they're waiting for a response. "I'm wondering if . . ."

"What?" Nina asks impatiently.

"How will we know the way people react to our slogans if we're not there to hear what they say?" She flashes on Johnny, who would no doubt walk by muttering something about vandalizing private property.

"Interesting point." Ben nods.

"You should've brought it up yesterday," Nina says. "It's dangerous for any of us to return now."

"Of course," she agrees quickly, unwilling to cause upset. These are her new friends. She wants to remain in their good graces.

-5-

After bathing in scented water, Celia wraps her body in the silky robe Paul brought home from his one gig in France. Would she feel such anticipation if he were here all the time? Is that the message of their marriage, young together forever with stories galore to share? No one she knows who has been married as long as she has waits eagerly for a visit from her husband.

They met at a sweet sixteen party and danced together all night. Then drove in his old car to a spot under the Whitestone Bridge to watch the sun come up. When she got home, her mother was livid, wouldn't stop going at her. She told her mother not to worry; they were going to get married. Ten months later, they did. She'd just turned seventeen.

When she checks the time, which she's been avoiding, it's nearly 1:00 p.m. On the phone last night, he said, "See you around nine in the a.m. tomorrow. I'm aching, baby."

But when was Paul ever on time? Still, precious hours alone together are ticking away. It won't be long before her sons arrive home from school.

If the band encountered problems, Roper would've phoned her. He looks after Paul, who's too wired to look after himself. Paul is always fighting his way out of some mental fray, which takes energy, conviction, and imagination. His black eyes are lit by a fuse so fierce he appears a little crazed. He's her proof, though, that excitement reigns, that risk is rewarded, and that there's always a possible shine to a dull day. More than husband, lover, father, he represents a credo: anything can happen, baby, and it will be far out. Without that, it's all a deep plod.

"Where's Pop?" Quincy calls from the vestibule, Sam behind him.
"Late."
"What do you think happened?"
"Traffic. Car trouble. Don't know." Sam leans into her. "Hey, my guy, how was school?"
"Okay," he whispers.
"Are you worried?" Quincy asks.
"A little."
"Miles will know what to do."
"I'm glad you think so."
"Pop's not usually this late." Quincy has the innate ability to speak her fears aloud.
"It's only a few hours. Let's not fret too much yet."
"When will you begin to worry a lot?"
"Quince, that's a silly question."
"Not the way I see it. Worry is like mercury. When it begins to climb, you have to do something, or it'll burst the thermometer. So if Pop's not here by five, and that's eight hours late, we'll have to do something about it."
"Yes, we will. Take Sam into the kitchen for a snack. You're scaring him." And me, she thinks.
"Here's what I believe," Quince continues. "Pop got his dates wrong. He never looks at a calendar. I bought him the five-year datebook last Christmas. He forgot to take it with him. It has no value to him if he leaves it on the dresser."
"You're right, sweetie."

Miles comes into the room, drops his book bag on the floor. "Where's Pop?"

"We don't know. He's late."

"Did he phone?" Miles asks her.

"Nope." The dark promise of rain enters the room. She switches on a lamp.

"He knows you're waiting," Miles says. His eyes are as deep and dark as his father's.

"Yes, he does."

"Did you call the other guys in the band?" Miles asks.

"Just about to."

"I'll do it." Miles's take-charge attitude is comforting. First-borns grow up fast. She did.

He dials Roper's number. No answer. After three more calls to other band members with no success, he says, "Maybe there's been an accident."

"Mom, phone Uncle Johnny. He can track Pop's van." Quincy tugs at her hand as if to pull her to her senses.

"Johnny," she mumbles. That isn't a path she wants to follow, but her sons need action. How can she say that Paul could be high and hanging out at some roadside bar? If Johnny does track him to any such place, her family will start talking rehab and never stop. No, she doesn't want her brother involved. "Listen guys, let's give it until eight before . . ."

The phone rings.

Quincy reaches for it. "Pop, where are you? We're worried."

She watches her son's face as he listens, then hands her the receiver.

"One of the band members became ill. We're in some emergency room in Albany. Baby, I'll be there tomorrow."

But she can't take another sick day.

6

From the telephone booth, Josie can see the VW in the rest area, her friends inside waiting impatiently. For the last few hours, riven by indecision, she's had this phone call on her mind. Tonight is her brother's farewell party. But taking action against the war is what it's all about now. Going to a party instead of an antiwar protest would be indefensible. Anyway, how would she explain such a decision to her friends?

She dials home. The phone rings a few times.

"Hello." Richie's sleepy voice.

"Sorry I woke you. About tonight, I won't be back in time for your party."

"Where are you?"

"On the highway to DC, going to an antiwar demonstration. What time do you leave tomorrow?"

He mumbles the hour, but it's clear he wants to go back to bed.

"I'll go with you to Port Authority."

"No, don't want that."

She imagines his forehead resting against the kitchen wall. "Are you sure?"

"Sure."

"Richie, I'm sad about missing tonight," and she is, more deeply than she anticipated. "Please. Don't forget to write."

"Okay. Bye." He hangs up.

With the dead line still at her ear, she laments not having said something more personal. But what could that have been?

Ben is driving, Lowell beside him. The rolled-up windows do little to keep out the cold winter air as she huddles in the back seat between Nina and Maisie. Empty coffee containers and gum wrappers litter the floor. They've been driving for several hours now.

"Look at all the cars," Ben says. "A million people going to protest. LBJ, pay attention, man. We're coming to get you. Ooh ooh."

"He's real scared," Nina says. "I hope you're not basing your assessment on a traffic jam."

"You're no Mary Poppins."

"And you shouldn't mix reality with fantasy."

"A little joke helps the medicine go down," Ben mutters.

"Reality dictates we see the actual size of the demonstration before we speculate on numbers."

"One million, fifty thousand, thirty thousand, it's still a clear message," Maisie says. "We keep this up, and LBJ *will* have trouble sleeping."

"A clear message?" Lowell says, pouncing on her words. "People have been at this protest shit for a good while, and what do we have? More body bags. The government doesn't care if we parade around Washington. They don't care if we stay up all night chanting slogans. They don't care if we paint designs on our cheeks or on their buildings. They don't care. We have to make them care."

"A little hash in their four o'clock tea," Ben mumbles.

"Get serious," Lowell admonishes.

"I am," he says. "I'm picturing the buttoned-up scions of government dancing wildly."

"More troops, bombs, deaths, more concentrated destruction than anyone can defend." Lowell stares straight ahead.

Listening to his words, Josie once more offers up a prayer that Richie not end up in Vietnam.

"It's too early to dismiss the effectiveness of mass demonstrations," Nina says.

"I agree," Ben says. "These guys want to be reelected."

"Reelected? Senator A, Senator B, what does it matter? It's about influence, power, and who controls the military," Lowell says. "We have to make them pay a steep price each time they escalate the war. It's the only way."

What exactly Lowell wants them to do, he never explains.

"Demonstrations get people involved," Maisie says.

"LBJ and his cronies believe that white middle-class students, who benefit from the rewards of the system, are not going to cause real trouble. We need to teach them a lesson about us," Lowell says.

"I hear your frustration." Maisie ever the mediator.

"It's not about *our* frustration. It's about causing enough trouble in the US to make it harder for them to continue in Vietnam. What about you, Josie? Why don't you weigh in here?" Lowell glances at her.

"Is that the price of my ticket?" she quips. In a way, though, it is. Sometimes being together can feel like such a free-for-all, getting high, laughing, music playing, merriment ruling. At other times, her difference from them is apparent and even uncomfortable. Last night at the apartment there weren't enough beds for the four of them. Lowell and Ben insisted on sleeping on the floor because so many people in the world have it rough. It was as if they wanted to suffer. Try explaining that to her father.

She flashes on tonight's farewell party. Her father will close the restaurant early. Paul's at home and will be there along with Celia and their sons; so will Johnny and Terry. Only she will be missing.

Jingle-tingling tambourines, slapping and thumping drums, huge banners that blow in the breeze to graze heads and wrap faces, a cacophony of singsong voices. It's a sea of people. The energy, noise, the sheer reality of the event is overwhelming. Her step quickens with the electricity of excitement. There's magic here, a great human wave rising. Lowell is wrong. Numbers matter.

Police are everywhere: on the streets, on steps, in cars, and in vans that line the curbs. Only the cobalt-blue sky is unrestricted. As the snaillike march passes government buildings, she takes in the magnificent structures.

Suddenly, Lowell, Nina, and Maisie peel away from the march.

"Where are they going?" she asks Ben.

"People are spinning off to protest at the Justice Department. They've arrested some Black guys for I'm not sure what. Come with me." Ben tugs her down a side street filled with shouting, angry demonstrators.

Fists are up in the air; rhythmic words taunt the cops. A shiver of fear goes through her.

The crowd feels unruly, and her friends are quickly swallowed up and disappear from sight. Something in her wants to turn around, leave. But Ben still holds her hand as they continue to weave deeper into the crush till it seems there's no room to take another step forward.

Police with bullhorns are calling for them to disperse, warning they have no permit to be on this street. Mopeds rev up and start to circle; helicopter blades beat at the sky.

A phalanx of police dive into the crowd, faces smudged behind plastic shields, billy clubs erect. The crowd becomes a moving object. Ben is no longer holding her hand. A cop grabs the arm of a man beside her and brings down his club again and then again. "Stop!" she screams, her arm snapping between the man and the club, startling herself and the cop long enough for the man to leap away.

A cold fist of terror urges her escape. Gray smoke now clouds the air. Her eyes burn. The thwack of wood against bone reverberates in her head. People are pushing in every direction. It's an ominous ballet. Ben is nowhere in sight. Desperate to return to the march but unsure how, she begins to retrace her steps. And brushes aside a sudden hot flash of anger at being left on her own.

Finally, breathless and shaken, she reaches the relative safety of the march, which still wends its snaillike way toward the Washington Monument rally.

"Hey, sister, thanks."

She looks into the stern face of a young Black man. He offers a hand of long tapered fingers, which she shakes. "Who are you?"

"Yeah, we all look alike. You jumped in, distracted that cop."

"I didn't see your face." But she does now. His cinnamon-color skin is pulled so tightly over sharp bones she doubts he can smile.

"And who are you?"

"Josie Russo."

"Melvin Curtis here."

"Are you okay?" She sees some blood on his jacket shoulder.

A dismissive nod. "Where you from?"

"New York City. You?"

"Just finishing at Howard U."

"A student?" she asks.

"Is that a problem?"

"Of course not."

"And you?"

"I work for a living."

"No wonder," he muses.

"Is that supposed to mean something?"

"A passing remark." His tone as tight as his skin.

"Did you come with a group?" she asks.

"Yes. Best thing to do at these functions, though can't find them now."

"I lost my friends too, and no idea where the car is parked."

"Your first demonstration?"

"Yes."

The Washington Monument is now up ahead with thousands of people packed tightly around it trying to keep warm while listening to the speakers at the rally. Melvin offers a canteen of water.

"I'm not thirsty."

"Wash your eyes with some. It's the same gas they use in Vietnam, same helicopters too. Soon, it'll be the same guns."

"We have to escalate too," she says, parroting Lowell.

He makes a sound low in his throat that could be a laugh.

"At least we're working on it," she insists.

"Right. Some people get arrested; others get beat."

"I have to find my friends."

"Hey, I'm here."

"With all due respect, that's not going to help me."

"I know the layout of the town and you don't."

"Layout?"

"DC looks big but it's a nod in the bucket. We can head toward the main parking lots, try to find your car, but I'd be surprised if we do. Might as well leave the rally. We can't hear a thing anyway."

He leads her through a bunch of side streets until they're out of reach of the demonstration and in an area of run-down houses. From their windows, people watch children play on cracked slate sidewalks. Dilapidated storefronts wear signs announcing what they once were. A few liquor stores with half-gated windows, a barbershop, and a beauty salon are open for business. "Is this where you live?"

"Why would you guess that?" he says.

"Can you just answer me?"

"Because everyone here is Black?"

"Yes." His responses are making her feel stupid.

"I live near the university."

"So why are we here?"

"We're avoiding the path of the march the way the march avoids the Black community."

She glances at his straight-line jaw raised combatively. "Would people want strangers parading through their streets?"

"Visitors need to experience the pleasure of seeing how people live. That way, they can return to Idaho, Iowa, or Montana with an education they can't get at home."

"I don't think it'd matter that much, to be honest."

"What wouldn't matter?"

"Just walking through the ghetto . . ."

"Hey, people eat, play, make love, pray, dance, curse, sing, get born, and die here. It's run down, old, shabby, but it's a neighborhood."

"I can see that."

"You can see what?" His anger flares like a candle flame.

"Are we fighting about something?"

"A point of view. Take it on," he says.

"To please you?"

"Yeah, why not?" But she can hear he's lost interest, and that's fine with her.

"How far to the parking lots anyway?"

"That would be a royal waste of your time."

"Walking home to New York would be more of a waste."

"How about I take you to the Greyhound station and you get on a regular old bus to New York?"

Shit. She only has a few dollars, not enough for bus fare. "How much would a ticket cost?"

"We'll find out." He takes tight hold of her elbow, which startles her. Even more surprising is how much she wants him to hang on.

"I know money is in short supply, but could I borrow some for a ticket? I'll return it by mail tomorrow."

"Can do."

"Thanks, Mel."

"Not Mel, never Mel. Melvin."

"I could call you Mr. Curtis."

"You could."

7

Celia's on the couch with her legs stretched across Paul's lap when she hears the front door open and close. "We're in here."

"Hey, I'm home." Miles saunters in, his hair long to his shoulders.

"Sam's at a friend's. Quince is in the room studying, already preparing for West Point," she says.

"Doesn't his fixation on attending a war factory bother you?" Miles asks. "It's a war college. Why would he want to train to kill people?"

"He says he doesn't want to be drafted, wants to control his future. That he'd rather deal with it as an officer and issue the orders. He's sure it's a wiser course than the one Richie is following. Anyway, not to worry. By the time Quince is ready to go, the war will be over," she says.

"You don't know that. How can you be so apolitical?"

"Hey, my man, your mom likes the West Point idea, free haircut, neat uniform, no tuition, and lifetime referral. Run it by, check out the benefits."

Miles stares at his father, no doubt seeing the dilated pupils, the unshaven face.

"Son, keep the home fires fed tonight. I want to take your mom out dancing. She won't leave her babies alone."

"You just want company in some seedy place where you can listen to jazz," she teases. The only reason she agrees to spend hours in smoky, damp cellars with sealed windows is her hope that someone might recognize Paul and pull him up on stage. It'd give him renewed belief in his music.

"Your mother needs to experience my rhythms, dig?"

"Whatever you say, Pop."

It isn't hard to see that every word out of his father's mouth disturbs Miles. He's told her that Paul's talk is yesterday's hip and so phony he'd like to stuff cotton in his ears.

"Tell your old man about entering college. The teachers a bunch of guys with glasses halfway down their noses?"

"I just got there, didn't I?"

"Hey, handsome, don't get in a dander. I'm asking you to share. It's what a father does."

"How many of those have gone down cold?" Miles points to a few empty beer bottles.

"Working men drink during off hours. Don't you know what gives pleasure to this sour life?"

"I know you leave the sour life whichever way you can."

"Miles, enough," she says softly.

"Mom, there's a share in an apartment in Harlem near City College. A room has come empty. It'd be easier if I stayed there. I can pay three quarters of the rent from my part-time job and wondered if you could help me with the rest."

"You ask, we give." Paul's head falls back on the couch.

"Mom?"

She swings her feet to the floor. "I don't know, Miles."

"Why not?"

"Can I squeeze any more out of my paycheck? Then, too, Harlem. I'll worry about you every night."

"Lots of students live there. And people are people, for God's sake. It's fine when Black guys fight in the war to save your ass but not okay for your son to live in Harlem. Christ, Mom, I thought you were different."

"I'm not being racist. But crime is crime, and we know where it's happening. Every Black mother would like her son out of Harlem."

"You don't know what you're saying, and you can't imagine how upset it makes me. I'll take on another part-time job for the difference. I can't stay here anymore."

"Miles, why?" But she knows why. He can't watch his father waste away while his mother seems to turn a blind eye.

"I need the privacy," Miles says, avoiding her gaze.

"You won't slack off studying, will you?"

"If I do, they'll draft me."

"That's not why you're in college."

"It's the way I see it right now. Too many people dying hourly for nothing I agree with."

"Paul, please. Say something."

"You can't keep a man where you can see him just to see him." Paul's voice is light, thin, nothing to hold on to.

"Mom? The rent? Can you help?"

"Yes, okay, we'll manage something."

"Thanks. I've got to do some reading. See you later."

"Miles, he's just growing up, a long weed." Paul strokes her hair. "Got to let him go, my lady. He's already burdened by life's woes."

"I know, but so much is happening in those streets. It's scary. I dread letting any of my sons out of sight."

"Hey, life will get at their brains whether they're here, there, or anywhere. They have to walk through to get through, see?"

"You worry me too, you know."

He continues stroking her hair. "That's a real waste of your time. Because no matter what, I'll do what I do, see?"

"You talk circles. What're you saying?" As long as she's known him, Paul has been sure of himself. He would do it. Whatever it was. She only needed to be there to watch. Lord knows, she did watch and still does, but what she sees now scares her.

"I exist because my heart beats; otherwise, no one to take to another planet with my music. I'm stuck in an elevator cage, and the piped-in music is theirs, not mine, and I'm not retrainable."

"All this morbid crap just to spook yourself. I know you better. It's not over. You'll make more music. It's in you. You're just scared of change. You've never had to adjust before. Now you do." She's afraid to let him go on, afraid he'll spiral down to a place too deep for her to rescue him. She stands, pulls at his arm until he swings his legs off the couch. "Let's go dance."

March 20

Dear Sister Josie,
Sounds religious, doesn't it? Remember the nun? She hated the boys. Liked you, though. Okay, so you want to know everything. I mean, it's basic training, manageable but prisonlike. My problem is I'm never alone, not in the barracks, the bathroom. On the grounds I'm marching, running, someone tagging alongside. In the mess it's elbow to elbow. At night, in bed, the guys talk in their sleep, and I swear their dreams mix in with mine to wake me. Not one of the NCOs, not one, speaks in a normal tone. They shout everything day and night. My eardrums are taking a bigger beating than my feet, which I'm told are not doing their job until the pain reaches my eyeballs. Food's bad, rubbery. Cooked too long. My tongue's beginning to swell from all the salt. Sounds awful but actually it could be worse. Our sarge has a sliver of heart (just a sliver) while most of the other NCOs are complete vultures who live off blood, sadists who get their jollies from driving the guys till they drop. Everything they shout has sexual content, it's bizarre.
Mainly, though, they're forcing (breaking) our bodies into shape and teaching us how to use guns, bayonets (scary), and other ways of killing. But the word they constantly throw at us is "endurance." I see their point. If we make it through this, and there's no guarantee everyone will, we'll be ready, although no one says for what. Words like "jungle," "gook," "Communist," but there are no picture books, so it remains X, the unknown.

I mean, I didn't expect paradise, and that's what it's always about, expectations. So if it's a decent day, I'm pleased but surprised, if it's a grind (most of the time), I take it in stride. What else can I do?

Rumor has it we'll get leave after basic, but another rumor says not. If we do, I accept your invite to crash at your new digs, which sound outstanding. That you can afford them even more outstanding. The girl's going up in the world. I received a letter from Celia, one from Miles (who vows never to serve), and a package from Terry, whose notes are so short they worry me. Is she all right? Anyone hear anything about Cousin Grace? Probably not or you would've told me. I'm not sure I need your blow-by-blow of every action against the war. Some of them sound more dangerous than boot camp. Anyway, I'm not going to comment on your comments about Nam. I'm not even sure these letters aren't read. I'm not really sure about much, except wanting out of Dix. That's their philosophy, work us to the marrow so no one in his right mind would ever want to spend an extra day here, and when it's time to leave, we're all going to fight to be first in line.

We're about to lockstep into the showers. Remember those movies about concentration camps? It gives me the creeps when all the water comes on at the same time.

So that's it for now. If you take care of yourself, I'll do the same.

Love,
Richie

PS: Who's this guy you're seeing? Sounds mysterious. Does he have a name? I mean, if you're spending so much good time with him, you must know it. Why would I mention him to anyone at home? Don't get paranoid.

-8-

Her fingers stroke Melvin's smooth, hard stomach. His body is splayed on the bed like Jesus on the cross. She's accused him of indifference after they make love, so he's trying to stay awake, but his eyes are drooping.

Though it's been many months, it continues to amaze her that he's here beside her in their own place, their relationship almost sudden. Though a phone call from him was highly improbable, she slipped in her phone number when she mailed the money she owed him.

Not long after, he phoned that he was in New York. That she'd been heavy on his mind. Did she want to see him? She said yes at once. He'd been on her mind since the day they'd met.

All through the spring, with him on scholarship at Columbia and her at work, they spent nearly every evening together. His curiosity about her is as endless as his approval. Both are reciprocal. Their favorite haunt is an old bar on Broadway, though most nights they're the only interracial couple there. The people that traffic in and out look at them with interest or curiosity.

"Do you want to leave?" she asked on one of their first dates there.

"Why?" he said.

Racism, the war, and how to change society are always on the agenda. Their futures will be ones of devotion to the struggle. It's a given. Discussing families is more difficult. She's told him her family wouldn't be welcoming, because he's Black. But didn't say he'd be met with silence. It saddens her. He's said his mother thinks it's dangerous for him to be involved with a white woman. She responded to this by asking if *he* cared that she was white. He took a moment to respond, a moment in which she wished she hadn't asked. Then he asked if she cared that he was Black. She replied no, at once. But he never did answer her question.

They laughed past the fact that they weren't virgins. Where she grew up, a virgin over the age of fifteen was deemed an outcast, information she didn't share. He'd had a few girlfriends, he admitted. She didn't probe, though did wonder if any of them had been white. None of it matters. She can barely contain her happiness and says so. He, too, says that he's gladder than he's been since he was a little kid riding a bike in the wind, which he equated with freedom to be, to just be.

"Being together is a daily blessing," she whispers, and wraps her arm around his neck.

"Ease up on the choke hold," he mumbles.

"Let's walk to the cappuccino place."

"You're mad, girl. That's nearly three miles."

"Loving you fills me with restless energy."

"Yeah, baby, well, the act of loving you leads me to contemplation."

"About what?"

"Why did I know you'd ask? The memory of filling you refills me. Get it?"

"You're full of royal shit." She crosses her arms behind her head, stares at the ceiling, content. Both of them are busy with political activities as well as work and school. Today, however, she called into work sick and he cut classes. They had all afternoon together. "Know what the movement lacks?"

"You're going to tell me."

"A union. If we had a union, we'd have holidays, bonuses, maybe even vacations."

"After the revolution."

"Melvin, there's not going to be a revolution, not the kind that happened in Cuba or China."

"So what are we fighting for?"

"Change, major change."

"Not good enough, baby. Or maybe good enough for your middle-class white friends. They need a fix of morality to go on doing their lives. For us coloreds, honey child, everything must be uprooted, turned around, renamed, reset. It's a matter of life or death." He yawns.

"I agree, but it'll come in stages, not one full sweep. There's no Winter Palace to . . ."

Propping herself up on her elbow, she sees his eyes close. Even in repose his face doesn't relax. A tiny muscle beneath his cheek trembles like a trapped moth. He's told her that growing up in the South taught him to never sleep deep. Though study has kept him grounded these past months, he's aching to break out, to be in the streets, to organize to *make* it happen. Miles, who hates the war with a passion, feels the same way. She shares their impatience.

Endless meetings in rooms so smoke filled she might as well take up the habit try her patience. Instead of engaging in infinite debate to reach a consensus on simple decisions, they should be organizing on city streets, country roads, in Laundromats and suburban malls, talking nonstop to any passerby about racism and about the unlawful war where she fears Richie will land.

She taps Melvin's forehead. "Don't sleep."

"Can't not."

"Get up and walk with me."

"Hey, girl, I'm not drunk, just tired. Don't you know I love you even when I'm asleep?"

Actually, she does. Tenderness and admiration come easy to him, and he never stints on the words to express them.

"I love you too," she says, and presses her face into his chest. He strokes the back of her head.

When the phone rings they look at each other. "You get it," she urges.

"Says nothing anywhere about having to answer every call," he mutters, swinging his long legs off the bed.

"What?" he says. His suddenly tense body alerts her. "I'll be there." He hangs up and begins pulling on his pants.

"What? What is it?"

He looks at her. Bewilderment crosses his face. It's as if he doesn't recognize her.

"What, Melvin? Tell me."

"Martin Luther King's been shot."

"Dead?"

He nods. "Shot by a white guy."

"Oh no." She reaches for her jeans.

"Where you going?" His tone as distant as the planet Mars.

"Melvin, please, I want to go with you. I can't wait here and do nothing. I want to shout and fight." It's her loss too, she doesn't say.

"What you want and what's possible are not identical. I'm going up to Harlem. It'll be dangerous there. I'll phone you."

He's out the door, leaving a vacuum of silence behind. Did something decisive just happen, something apart from King's death? Did Melvin dismiss her help because she's white, or because she's female, or because it's Harlem? Was he protecting or rejecting her? Only she can't dwell on that now. Important tasks are at hand. She must find her own way to fight the deplorable killing. Someone has to pay. She saw it in Melvin's eyes. Though even with brown skin, he's not safe up there tonight. The cops will be all over Harlem. He's wearing only a windbreaker. What kind of protection is that?

A cacophony more insistent than the noise of a jet plane enters through the open window. She looks out to see a posse of Black teenagers marching up Broadway, beating ashcan covers with sticks. The man who killed Dr. King was white, like her. Tonight, she's not welcome to join them.

She switches on the TV. The faces of reporters morph into the faces of Memphis officials, government representatives, white men all. She dials Miles's number.

"I know, I know," he says.

"Melvin's on his way to Harlem. He wants me to wait here. Jesus, how can I? It's maddening. I'll take the train to your place. It's closer to—"

"No, don't. The guys in my room are making plans to do our own thing."

"Oh. Okay. Talk to you later." As soon as she hangs up, the phone rings.

"Did you hear?" It's Maisie.

"Yes. Melvin is on his way to Harlem. Where are you?"

"Nina and I just got home."

"I'll be right there. Gather everyone. We have to respond."

The phone rings again. "Maisie?"

"You little shit."

"What?"

"You haven't called home in weeks."

"Johnny?"

"You little shit."

"You want to say something, say it fast. I'm about to hang up."

"Pa's in Bronx-Lebanon Hospital. He had a heart attack."

She runs three never-ending blocks to the subway. An ashy darkness has replaced the April sunlight. The station is empty, the token booth closed. Ducking under a turnstile, she paces the platform. She'll go to the hospital after the meeting at Maisie's. Heart attack doesn't mean instant death. Her family, especially Johnny, view any health problem as if death is the next step. Her father is in a hospital. He's being taken care of. Dr. King, though, is dead. The note she scribbled to Melvin said nothing about her father. She doesn't want him showing up at the hospital; her family will not be friendly.

The apartment door is ajar, the air inside filled with cigarette smoke. The TV is on, the volume low, but no one is watching. It's been a while since she's been here. Everything looks the same except that now about fifteen people are seated on chairs and the floor. She steps over some pillows and finds a space on the floor beside Ben.

"Pretty awful, isn't it?" he says.

"It is."

Ben slides an arm around her shoulder. "Want a toke?"

"Not now." What she wants now is a short meeting so she can get to the hospital. No one in her family would ever understand the decision to come here first. Though her mother will pointedly say nothing and Celia little, Johnny will announce her absence on the hour perhaps to the distress of her father.

"Dr. King came out against the war. It's why he was killed," Maisie states.

"What're you proposing?" someone asks.

"A leaflet to explain this."

"To distribute where?" Nina asks.

"The campuses."

"Students already know this crap. Try the streets," Josie says, her impatience hard to disguise.

"It's not enough," Lowell says.

"Let's take over a radio station, demand twenty-four hours devoted to Dr. King."

"Feels odd for white people to do it."

"We need to let them lead."

"Them? Like we're the adults?" Josie's tone too harsh by far.

"It's just semantics. Cool it," Ben says.

Cool it? How can she? Her father sick, and Melvin, is he even safe? What if he ends up in a hospital as well?

"Let's find out if there are already plans in the works," Nina says.

"Yes," Josie says. "Meet with Black leaders, see what they need us to do, and then bring up the radio station action."

"She's right," Lowell says. "I can get in touch with one of the Black leaders and bring back any message."

She leans over and whispers, "Ben, let me know the final details. I have to split now."

In the quiet hospital lobby, a man lounges on a worn couch, while another sleeps in a large chair. A middle-aged Black woman sits behind the information desk. I'm so sorry Dr. King is dead, she doesn't say. I loved and respected him.

"My father, Anthony Russo, is a patient here. He had a heart attack. I know it's past visiting hours, but I came straight from the airport. I'm a student in Michigan." If they give her a hard time, she'll refuse to leave. It's her father. She has a right to see him no matter what time it is.

The woman's eyes scan a sheet of names. "I'll find someone to help you."

She settles into the nearest chair. Promises herself that after her father recovers, she'll stay more in touch with him. He came to mind when she was reading a book about alienated labor. He likes to hear her talk. She'll explain why all his years at the leather factory before the restaurant felt so oppressive and why he collapsed at his workstation. That it wasn't his weakness, as he believed, but a sane response to an intolerable situation. She wants to illuminate his understanding and lighten his burden the way that knowledge is lifting hers.

The woman beckons her to the desk.

"Doctor on call is Wilson. He'll meet you on the sixth floor. Take a pass."

She finds a bank of elevators. Waits forever until one arrives.

The elevator doors open on a silent, empty gray lounge with a wall telephone and several plastic chairs. A man in a white coat heads toward her.

"Russo?"

She nods.

"Dr. Wilson. So awfully sorry to be the one to . . ."

Her eyes take him in as if he were made up of tiny particles held together by a strange substance that she needs to discover: white hair, dark eyes, gray moustache, wrinkled cheeks, large chin, creased neck, long arms, and black shiny shoes. He continues to talk, and the sounds bounce around outside her brain. She remembers the black-lined mouths on TV and their useless words.

"Where's my father now?" she interrupts.

"On the way to the chapel of your family's choice."

The doctor extends his hand, but she's already at the exit door.

At home the note to Melvin is where she left it.

It's after two; she can't call her family. She'll phone Celia at seven. She'll phone work as well, tell the supervisor her father has died, that she'll be out for several days. Why does it feel like a lie? As the country laments the loss of Martin Luther King, there seems no room tonight for her father's death.

Once she attended a friend's cousin's funeral and watched everyone cry. She faked a sad face; it seemed the right thing to do. It wasn't her cousin. But it is her father. Gone. Forever. How does anyone deal with that? The senseless deaths in Vietnam often move her to tears, make her angry, and that fury drives her to action. Now her grief is too sudden, deep, and private to move her in any direction. Please, Melvin, she prays, come home soon.

She switches on the radio news and sits on the bed listening. The DJ says there's rioting in Harlem. People are probably tearing up the streets, teargas everywhere. A minister is saying that rioting isn't what Dr. King would want, that there's a better way. But is there? Rage needs an outlet. People have been throwing things inside their houses for years. Now the frustration has gone outdoors.

The newscaster predicts that the rioting will end with the night. It won't. It's about more than Dr. King's death. It's about life, which continues, except for her father, who was too tired to wait for change.

Josie enters the Bronx Zoo through the hidden alley-slim path. She begins to climb the hill to their sanctuary. In a while, she and Miles will head to the chapel where the rest of the family will gather. After the viewing, black-suited men will carry the coffin into the nave where the priest will offer words that reflect nothing real about her father. He hoped to transform his past into their great futures. How could he have known that his chances were minimal? If he'd stayed in the old country, he would've been poorer but maybe happier. At least he wouldn't have had to adjust to the ways of strangers. Too late to reassure him that her life will be different, because isn't that what he wanted?

It's early; there are no visitors yet. The kiosks are shuttered, the cafeteria as well, tables upended, chairs piled in corners. In an hour or two, children from nearby schools will come and toss peanuts to the animals, missing the creatures by a mile. She never enjoyed the school trips to the zoo. Sad-eyed animals staring helplessly past fences or pacing paths that never lengthened, entering caves that never deepened. It shamed and terrified her.

The cloudless sky is unbearably blue, though it's not a great day. Many inner cities are burning. Still no word from Melvin; he was gone all night.

Miles breaks through the nearby brush behind her. Together

they follow a snaking path around clumps of bushes to reach the slate-smooth surface of their rock with its jagged edge that juts over the tree line. From that vantage point, they can see the rectangle of park, the scaffolding for a new motel on Southern Boulevard, and down into the neighborhood where she grew up. Up here, she's lost to family while they're within her sight, the anonymity sweet.

What if she and Miles remained on the sun-striped rock heating slowly beneath them till the funeral was done?

"Grandpa gone, it's hard to believe." His voice deep, soothingly familiar.

"So much I wanted to tell him that might've made him feel better about himself."

"Like what?"

"He never understood his exploitation, or he wouldn't have been so hard on himself."

"He wasn't a worker. He owned a pizza store."

"There's more than one kind of worker, Miles. He slaved in that factory for years before ending up on his feet for fifteen hours a day."

"I'll tell you something, my father is next to go."

"Jesus, do you want to say more?"

"No."

"I haven't had any word from Melvin. It's the first time he's been away all night."

"I heard from Lowell that a group of Black brothers plans to take over some Columbia buildings," he says.

"Will Melvin be with them?"

"Don't know. They'll protest King's death and university plans to build a gym in the midst of a third-world community."

"Who told you this?"

"Lowell brought two brothers to crash on our floor last night."

The men have met, she thinks bitterly. "I need to find Melvin. Will you come with me to Harlem?"

"We have a retreat. I'm leaving after the burial."

"Retreats are for Catholics, not collectives. What's going on?"

He shrugs. "Stuff."

A few clouds wander into view.

"How well do you know the guys in your collective?"

"You keep asking me that," he accuses, which annoys her because much of his education results from her activities.

"Anyone could be a provocateur."

"Josie, that shit is spread around so we won't trust each other."

"Who are the people in your collective?" she persists.

"I can't say."

A weird loneliness enters her. "You can't say? Who do you think you are? Fidel?" But she's disappointed. He sounds like some of the movement men who hoard secrets like bonbons to distribute as favors.

"I swore to secrecy."

A flock of birds flies so high she can barely see their shapes. "Miles, think everything through." He always looked to her, curious to know her next steps. Now his collective seems to have more influence on him than anyone else, including her.

"Are you against serious action?" he asks.

"Not in principle, but white people aren't uncomfortable enough to support violence. I'm not saying that'll always be true. In Algeria people were miserable enough to appreciate any tactic. It'll take longer here." This isn't the conversation she wants to be having now. They should be talking about her father, his grandfather.

"What constitutes miserable enough? A war in our name that never ends? Catastrophic bombing? Killing innocents? Burning children? Destruction of a country? Planeloads of body bags? The deep pockets of Dow Chemical? Prisons filled with Black people? Jailing of welfare mothers? Packaged lies on a daily basis? And now Dr. King? What, Josie, what more?" He's not challenging her, just reciting the litany of horrors they all carry around.

"Violent actions would be bad before a majority of people are won over to our thinking." But her words feel old and brittle; a mere tap would shatter their surface.

"Every revolution employs diverse tactics," he says.

"If we up the ante right now, what will we accomplish?" she asks.

"End the war? How's that for achievement?"

"You don't know that. What about the new way of life we talk about nonstop?"

"That struggle goes on too," but he sounds uninterested.

Climbing the steps to the apartment, her father's stone-cold cheek is still on her lips. Except it wasn't her father. It was a dressed-up body. And now more than ever she longs for his gentle warmth. About thirty people filled the church pews. Miles sat with his arm around Celia, who was sobbing. Terry held Johnny's hand in her lap. Richie's absence was palpable. Only she and her mother sat in mute pain, releasing none of their grief.

She fishes in her bag for the keys. Her plan is to change into jeans, then go up to 125th Street. Maybe someone at the Liberation Bookshop will have information about Melvin's whereabouts.

Entering the apartment, she hears the shower. Then pounds on the locked bathroom door. "Melvin, it's me." In seconds, the door flies open, and his wet body wraps hers. "I know, baby, your father. I heard. Damn, damn, sorry. It'll be okay. Real sorry." So tight against him, she's as wet as he is.

"Where've you been?" she mumbles, her face pressed to his chest.

He dances her back till they fall onto the bed. Then he rocks her, crooning, "Sweet honey, sweet baby," her cheek nestled in his damp, soap-scented neck. She feels him getting hard, murmurs, "No," needing to remain entwined, his whispered words soothing her agony as the late-day sun torches the room.

She's still riding the edge of a floating sadness when her eyes open on the flickering shadows in the room from the neon lights below. The cloying scent of the funereal lilies is still with her. Except for Miles, they all went to Celia's place after the burial. No one talked about her father. Instead they talked about the funeral. She didn't stay long. Couldn't. Worried about Melvin, she ached to go find him. And how much of the night will he share with her? He's a talker but selective in what he communicates. When she says as much, he either shrugs or teases about her nonstop curiosity, depending on his mood. Still, she can't help but wonder if he'd be more forthcoming if she were Black. When she starts thinking that way she does the only thing she can do, loves him even harder.

"Melvin?" she whispers, then slides an arm around his back. Awake, he rolls over to face the ceiling.

"People are meeting up at the university at dawn," he says more to himself.

My father just died, she wants to remind him.

"Not me, though. I'm done there." His flippant tone unlike his usual grave self. "Can't sleep. I'm getting some coffee." He slips out of bed, fills the kettle, and washes some cups, his movements too energetic for this time of night. Is it excitement?

"What happened in Harlem last night?"

"Fire, broken glass, sirens, screams, shouts, curses, rage, and glee. People's feelings ran the gamut from 'I don't give a shit about any of it' to 'This land is my land too.' All of it taking place within barricades and TV lights and cameras everywhere as if Harlem itself was a movie set. I considered grabbing a few pots and pans but didn't want to carry them around. The cops were swinging clubs like it was a golf course."

A white woman there would've been an impediment to him. How many times will she have to stay behind? Suddenly anxious about what else she doesn't know she slips out of bed to join him. In the predawn sky, only a sliver of light.

"Want some coffee?"

"Sure. It sounds like a repeat of last summer's riots, people beaten, arrested and nothing going forward."

"True. People's anger needs to be focused into a force that makes a long-term difference." He pours boiling water over the instant coffee.

"You weren't running in the streets for all hours of the night. So what else was going on?"

He stares into the coffee cup, considering. His face wears an expression she doesn't recognize. "Well, it's the way it is, Josie, the way it has to be, baby. We're going to open a Panther office on One Twenty-Fifth. That's it. I'm part of the solution."

"Columbia?"

"Not first on the list anymore. Doesn't matter. Once the caucus takes over university buildings, my scholarship is blown. And that's okay. I can finish my master's whenever. Now, though, we have to find a storefront, get a newspaper out, programs started, politics sorted, including our relationship to white groups like SDS. So you asked and I'm telling. That's what's happening." He takes a tentative sip of the coffee, stretches back his neck but doesn't look at her.

"How long have you been sitting on this idea?" The wall calendar is still on January, a forest dark with pine trees.

"After running the streets for a while, I spent the rest of the night with a group of like-minded brothers and sisters."

A stab of jealousy she will not give in to. "Care for my input?"

"Of course." Although naked, he looks weirdly invulnerable.

"Liar."

"Well, it's this way, Josie. I mean, events create needs, which have to be dealt with. You say that all the time."

"Melvin, once you begin work in Harlem, the cops will be all over you."

"Yeah, I think so."

"And you could get drafted."

"No matter, I'm not going."

"You sound so calm. Why?"

"Because I'm not you?"

"Wrong answer, smartass."

"And the right one . . .?" he asks.

"Establishing an organization, programs, newspapers, lord, it's postrevolutionary. It's not going to be a breeze. Difficult tasks need extraordinary preparation to complete." But what she wants to say and can't is that she fears being left out of all of it.

"Look and listen, Josie. Black people are dying on a daily basis from too many events they have no control over, including this war. Whatever we do we need to do fast. Whatever parts succeed will be fantastic. Whatever fails won't be worse than what exists. Get it?"

"Don't be pissed. I'm not against your plan." Something, though, is disturbing her breathing.

June 25

Dear Josie,
    You'll never guess the view outside my window. Mountains of snowy-white cloud. Could be Siberia. Just an hour ago it was all pink cotton candy. I'm in a huge commercial plane over the Pacific. The distance from nose to tail is longer than our neighborhood. Quick stops in Hawaii and Okinawa before landing in notorious Nam. My new address remains a closely guarded secret. Something to do with security, but we believe the brass can't make up their minds. First we hear Da Nang, then south near Cambodia. Anyway, none of it means anything. Jungle is jungle.
    The stewardesses actually hang out, want to know where we're from, got a girlfriend, stupid questions like that, but they're so alive and pretty, who cares? They cater too. Would Prince Richie like a hot towel for the back of his neck? More writing paper? Another helping of chocolate cake? More Coke? They can't serve booze, but we all knew to bring our own, so by flask, thermos, and plain old jar, we're drinking it up while eating steak and potatoes. More than a few final-meal jokes.
    Leaving Fort Polk (Tiger Land) (jungle training) was bliss. Remember school fire drills? About as far from what'd happen in a real fire as a person could get. I hated every humid day at Polk. SO BORING!!!! Funny thing is, moving through all the little shit camps between Jersey and Texas, I never felt I was away. More like wandering with no sense of being anywhere. That's about to change.

I'm kind of blown away by how far from home I'll be. We're passing through eleven or twelve time zones. Can you imagine? That much distance is bound to change the way home looks, which is good, which you understand, I know, so I won't explain further.

My last letter ignored your questions because you ask too many, they get intrusive. Besides I needed to let it sit there like one of Terry's stews. God I don't miss those. You're right. I could've gone to the funeral on a pass. I phoned Ma to say I didn't want my squad to take off without me. Truth is I couldn't deal with the tears, and with Pa already dead, being there didn't make sense. I see him in front of me all the time, but I can't hear his voice. Is that weird? You're right he was a depressed man. But you lose me when you say there could've been a better way. You apply some strange framework to questions, which passes me by. I agree he worked hard with little satisfaction. What else could he do? He had us. Maybe if he shared your dreams, he might've been less disappointed. But who knows? You don't, Josie.

You asked if I had an instinct about myself. What you meant was, do I think I'm going to die? I don't, but short of that it's a whole new problem. At home I always saw trouble coming, the way a guy walked, something in the eye, the voice, whatever, and usually I was right to duck, run, or grab a piece of pipe. What's upcoming, what trouble will look like, I can't say, and it does provoke sweat and palpitations. Will I be able to kill? The guys talk about it all the time, how everything's defensive in war, how being shot at changes morality, religious *beliefs, even the color of the sun. I hear that vets out of Nam still grapple with the concept. So time will tell, or not.*

Are you nuts? A coffee shop outside Dix? Have you dropped your marbles in the street? Have you ever seen Jersey State Troopers? Those bastards are over six feet and mean. Don't ask how I know. Do I think GIs will come in? Probably. Any civilized interaction is welcome during basic. But be careful what you say to the soldiers. You could confuse them. They might lose confidence. The army bends our brains into a belief system. You disturb that system, you're not helping anyone. See? Not that we buy everything we're told or even half, but we need to believe enough to get through the hot zones. What do you plan to say to a guy from Idaho? The war sucks, go home and go to jail? Trade your honorable for being a criminal? Yeah, free coffee, jive music, pretty faces, that'll please. But start banging away on how it's not worth dying for, etc. and so on, you're disturbing their peace. Think about it. Anyhow the place wouldn't last. No way the brass would tolerate the closeness of the coffeehouse. Free speech, what's that? So be ready. Or better yet open a café in the Village where we can all hang out when I return.

Celia writes lots of gossip about home but nothing about herself. Terry's notes couldn't be shorter, but she sends packages. Now, that's real nice. It's strange to think Pa's dead. I wish I could hear his voice.

From what you tell me, Melvin sounds pretty smart. And yeah, I understand completely about not sharing him with the family.

Josie, you'll do what you want no matter what I say, so be real careful and think.

Love,

Richie

PS: Remember the syrup over shaved ice that we slurped? I'm staring out the window at strawberry.

PART TWO

-10-

About to put the key in the lock, Celia notices the front door is slightly open. "Paul? Sam?" she calls. No response. She walks through the hallway to the bedroom, sees the half-open dresser drawer, and rummages inside. Her bracelets, necklaces, earrings, pins, barrettes, are there, but not her engagement ring. In Paul's underwear drawer, she checks for the cash she squirrels away in case of an emergency. It's gone; so, too, his underwear. In the closet his coat, leather jacket, and black suit, missing.

A dirty coffee cup, juice tumbler, and silverware in the kitchen sink mean that Paul left after Sam, who washes his breakfast dishes. She finds the leftover Merlot, pours it into a glass, and drinks it down quickly.

The phone rings. Miles rarely calls. Quince, at West Point, writes lovely letters that she stacks on the coffee table for anyone to read. Sam spends his after-school hours with Maria, a quiet child. Paul's saxophone case no longer leans on the living room wall.

She grabs her pocketbook off the chair where she set it down, dumps everything out on the table. No paycheck. Paul must've taken it during the night while she slept. He knew she couldn't get to the bank before tomorrow.

It happens. Men leave as if they were never there in the first place. Stories such as this are passed back and forth at work like descriptions of sitcom episodes: "Men don't like their lives, they take off." "Too much responsibility, they take off." Usually, there's speculation about younger flesh. Paul, however, is not in bed with another woman; he's in bed with drugs and getting high. High is the wrong description, he told her. It's not about rushes and energy. It's about being carefree, about letting go, abandoning time, existing in a state of zero anxiety, in short, nirvana. It's not that different from playing or composing music, he said. He's quite the professor on the benefits of smack. Now he can buy enough shit to OD. Is that what he wants? She won't pay for his funeral. Let them bury him in the potter's field.

The phone rings again. No doubt someone in her family calling to exchange the day's banalities. She's not ready to share.

There must be more wine in the pantry. Behind the olive oil is the red wine she uses for cooking. It tastes rancid; she drinks it anyway. Again the phone rings. She stares at the shiny black object. Perhaps it's Paul calling to apologize, saying he was out of his mind, has crashed, and needs a hand. Would she hang up? The phone stops ringing. She's the best thing that ever happened to him. Didn't he always say so? Didn't he whisper romantic lyrics, write music with her in mind? Didn't he always say how much he admired her, how he ached to be near her, that he loved her? Their membranes have been stitched together for so many years. How will she manage without that? Fuck!

No point crying, she admonishes herself through the sudden onrush of tears. What really hurts is the brilliant sky, each star cold and distant.

-II-

Josie replaces the receiver, upset that she couldn't find stronger words to console her sister. Sorry isn't ever enough. She cares about Paul. They all do. He's funny, engaging, and well meaning. When they were kids and playing in Miles's room, Paul would come in and sit on the top bunk and play the sax. She remembers the sounds as haunting, almost mysterious. And remembers as well feeling like a member of a privileged audience.

Now he's gone, deserted her sister. Maybe if there'd been enough money, Celia could've gotten him into some fancy drug addiction program. He'd never have gone to one of the free ones, prisonlike places that treat people like they're idiots. But just taking off? Her paycheck! That's unforgiveable and too awful to contemplate. Celia intends to tell the rest of the family, a deed Josie doesn't envy. Johnny will think it's Celia's fault even if he doesn't say so. What her mother might think, she wouldn't attempt to guess.

Though Celia's sorrow weighs on her, she must finish several tasks. On the kitchen table are several pounds of coffee, bags of cookies, and two large boxes of tea bags, all of which must be safely packed. Ben will drive the carton to the coffeehouse. People have given generously to the project. They were able to raise enough money for supplies and paint and . . .

The front doorbell sounds its emaciated ping. Through the

peephole, Nina's face peers back at her. "Just a minute." She frees the police lock that Melvin installed, which is heavier than a vault door to maneuver.

Nina, in tight jeans and gray silky shirt, tosses her jacket on the bed.

"Is everything okay?"

"We need to talk about . . . things," Nina says.

"Things?" She gazes at her friend's thin, molded face, which offers no clues.

"You never mentioned you had a brother in Nam."

"Why would I?"

"Don't be defensive,"

"I'll be anything I want."

"I guess I know less about you than I thought." Nina scans a bookshelf.

"Be more explicit, then maybe I can help you."

"This isn't some kind of trap, Josie, believe me."

"The Left inquisition?" It comes in like the tide but not as often, a sense of illegitimacy, of being judged. Unlike most others in the movement, she's neither a college student nor a high school graduate. And something about Nina's tone now makes it feel like high tide.

"You're acting silly."

"You're being devious," Josie says, and has a flash memory of junior high school. Her mother saying she dreamt that Josie had cut classes. It was true; she had. She realized later that someone must've told her mother. At the time, though, it had been ominous, her mother suddenly clairvoyant.

"Not sharing that your brother is a soldier when you're about to be in charge of the Fort Dix coffeehouse makes one wonder."

"Wonder what?" Whether Richie is a murderer of Vietnamese children? "My brother's in Nam, which doesn't make him a criminal."

"It's scary seeing you paranoid."

"What aren't you saying?"

"I was meeting with Melvin and some of the Panthers to discuss the upcoming march on Fort Dix. Melvin mentioned you were at home writing to your soldier brother and packing for the coffeehouse," Nina explains as if there's nothing more to say.

It occurs to her that maybe the visit isn't about her brother. "What was discussed at that meeting?"

"Just stuff we're trying to figure out."

"I hate the word 'stuff.'"

The tumbling of one lock after another stops the conversation.

"Hi," Melvin says.

"Hi." Her tone sullen.

"I came to learn more about Josie's views," Nina confides unhappily.

Melvin sees Josie's displeasure and grabs a piece of blank paper. Then slides an arm around her waist and prods her to the table. They sit side by side.

He writes: *We need to hide a carton in the coffeehouse with your permission.*

What's inside? she scribbles back.

Can't say, he writes.

Who does it belong to?

Can't say, he writes.

It's too dangerous, she writes wondering if Miles has anything to do with this, but won't ask.

Only for a few days.
What if we're busted?
It'll be well hidden, he writes.
So what? They can still find it.
It's only for a few days.
She can feel him trying to be patient with her. *How long exactly?*
It'll be stashed and retrieved while no one's there.
He scrunches up the paper, drops it in the sink, and lights a match to it.

"So you wanted to get a bead on my receptivity?" Josie says.

"I didn't do it well," Nina admits, grabbing her jacket. "I'll see you at the coffeehouse."

With his arm around her neck, they walk the empty streets to Riverside Park. It's late and it's cold. A sliver of moon plays hide-and-seek with the clouds. The strong wind coming off the river punishes the naked tree limbs.

On a bench outside the park, they sit close together, his warmth a promise.

"Tough visit with Nina." His tone gentle, wary.

She'd rather not discuss the topic except it's why they've come here.

"Nina's pussyfooting around freaked me. I wanted to chase her out with a broom the way my mother used to do with noisy kids at the restaurant."

"There's a line, sweet girl, between restraint and action, and we need to know when and how to cross it. Nina should've met you outdoors and shared. But she was concerned about how you'd react to the straight-out suggestion."

"Were you?"

"In a way." His tone cautious. "Certain situations demand risk. This is one of them." He stares ahead.

She glances at his resolute profile but says nothing.

"Important material has been secured. Someone is in the process of finding a safe hiding place. Right now the carton is stored in a car trunk, which is more dangerous than the coffeehouse."

"Are you involved in this?"

"Not at all. Just helping out a friend."

He's lying to her. To call him out on it would disturb the delicate space between his activities and hers. Already the struggle has changed from Black power to Black liberation, from antiwar to anti-imperialist, from resisting the state to taking it on.

"Melvin, you're in an organization that's being watched by the feds and the police all the time. Something happens, you'll have no second chance."

"I don't have the luxury of evaluating chances."

His serious tone warns of his new level of involvement. He often says that white people don't have the same skin in the game, a pun she dislikes. Still, the thought of letting him down pains her.

"Okay. Hide the carton in the coffeehouse. But don't think for a second that because I'm white, working class, I retain right-wing tendencies."

"Josie, am I sitting here with you or what?" His arm wraps her tightly, but he doesn't look at her.

12

The bus climbs a long, narrow hill. Josie exits at the last stop, which is the Fort Dix entrance. Used primarily by the army for basic training, the camp unfolds for miles. It's a short walk down a hill from the camp to the coffeehouse, which was once a storefront that housed a restaurant. Now the front plate-glass window is covered with posters of Ho Chi Minh, Che Guevara, Huey Newton, Dylan, Joplin, which afford some privacy, though the glass front door keeps visitors in sight. The coffeehouse faces a high bank of rock-embedded dirt, and in the distance terra-cotta roofs dot the landscape as if it's some ancient town.

She works at the coffeehouse on weekends and most evenings but manages the entire enterprise, which includes buying supplies as well as organizing people to be there. Entering, she hears Ron Jace strumming his guitar, his plaintive voice erratic as Ben fiddles with the speakers. Lowell, wearing a camouflage jacket over a T-shirt, sits with two GIs. Leila, the newest member in their coffeehouse collective, is listening in. Maisie leans against the wall talking to a soldier who looks too young to be a soldier. Nina is showing some magazine pages to an older man, and she wonders if he's from Fort Dix. Each face is engaged—a still life of devotion. She'd love to photograph the moment. Caption it: *We're doing all we can.*

She gets busy refilling supplies: stuffs two jars with peanut butter and ginger cookies, pours milk into the ceramic cow, and then replenishes a cup with quarters that allow soldiers to call home on the wall pay phone outside the back room. Earlier, she called Miles to ask if he could spend several hours at the coffeehouse. He said he was too busy. She asked him point-blank what was keeping him so preoccupied. "Too many things to enumerate," he replied, closing off further probing, which annoyed her. Does he even go to classes anymore? His only comment about his father taking off was that no one should be surprised.

She's sleeping here tonight to avoid waking at dawn to return for a delivery of chairs and other supplies. She forgot to leave Melvin a note. She'll phone him later. Like Miles, he hasn't spent any time here. She can vouch for the fact that he's busy around the clock with Panther business and often doesn't get home till two or three in the morning. She tries not to obsess about the new Harlem friends he tells her about, Rosemary and several others. It's petty to be jealous. Having such thoughts reminds her of the narrow thinking of some of the people she grew up with. When he does get home, he's too exhausted to talk; making love, though, that's another kind of energy.

A tall soldier in dress uniform enters and stands hesitantly near the door. She hands him a cup of coffee, introduces herself, and invites him to sit with her at a nearby table. He's Corey Selwyn from North Dakota.

"God, that's far," she says.

"I suppose." His voice deep.

"Just arrive?"

"Finished basic last week."

"Waiting?"

He nods. His gaze flicks past her to the others in the room. Men in ponytails, women in Gypsy skirts, different from North Dakota, she's sure.

"Have you gotten into the city?"

"I visited the Empire State Building. Everything's so tall."

"Even New Yorkers get dizzy looking up."

He smiles slowly and his cheeks dimple.

"How old are you?"

"Nineteen last month." He swipes at his hair, pale as a winter sun, though his complexion is ruddy. He hasn't touched the coffee.

"I bet you're homesick?"

"I miss the stars. Even on night patrol here, only a few are visible, no chessboards."

"Chessboards?"

"Come see what real night looks like, what a big sky can do."

"What can it do?"

"Float you through the universe on a diamond-studded carpet."

"How poetic," she says.

"Then you could meet my three border collies. They run for miles, then circle back."

"I've never had a dog."

"That's too bad."

"So how do you feel about the army?"

"It's different," he says.

"Different than what?"

"A lot of people living together with no time or space to wander around. I'd love to see what's on the far side of my barracks, take a long stroll through camp, but it's forbidden."

"I hear several soldiers disappeared after basic last week."

"There's talk about it, but everyone's more concerned about where we're headed next. I suppose Vietnam."

He makes Vietnam sound like a new word instead of the one etched in her brain. "My brother's in Nam right now." She rarely talks about Richie. Is superstitious that if she calls attention to him, the forces of the universe might seek him out to punish.

"Is that why you're doing this?" His chin points at the room.

"We opened the coffeehouse to talk about the war, to offer information so soldiers will learn there are other options than going to fight."

"What options?"

She shares with him some of Vietnam's history as well as how some men are refusing to be drafted, that there's a difference between military propaganda and what she and her friends are trying to do here, that their mission is to save lives, souls, and future self-respect.

"I'll probably be shipping out before there's time to absorb all that."

"Take some of our reading material. Guns aren't the only weapons; being armed with knowledge is good too."

"Do you talk the same way to every GI who comes in? I mean, are you always this serious?"

"I'm determined to do what I can to stop the war. One way to achieve that is if soldiers refuse to fight." Ron Jace's voice, smooth, melodic, filters into the space.

"You like to dance?"

"Yes, but it's not allowed here."

"Somewhere else, then?"

"I'm working. I can't."

"That's a true shame."

"Will you stop by again?"

"All depends on when I ship out, doesn't it?"

Exhausted, she locks the front door. Ben, also staying the night, will help her with the cleanup and with the delivery in the morning. The coffee urn needs to be washed, ashtrays emptied, the floor swept. All the stray paper cups bundled into bags with other trash. She sighs, begins to empty the urn of old coffee. Talking to Corey made her sad, his sweetness so uninformed. Maybe the coffeehouse isn't the best way to reach soldiers; maybe Richie was right that what she tells soldiers might be more upsetting than enlightening. She believes knowledge is power. But once they're in Nam, how much power does knowledge offer?

Ben props himself against the wall to roll a joint.

"Let's finish cleaning up first," she says.

"Hey, I'm productive when I'm high. Inhale, pick up trash, exhale, sweep. Who's the guy you sat with?"

"Corey. Could be I made a friend who might take another look at the war. Maybe. Who knows? That's just it. I'll never know. What about the soldiers you talked with?"

"One was really interested in some of the history. The other thought we were royal phonies. He asked if outside forces were sponsoring this coffeehouse bullshit. I told him he's off the mark, that my daddy's a Soviet, my mom is Chinese, so I would know." He flashes a wide smile of perfect white teeth.

"Do you believe everything you tell them?"

"Every damn syllable. Why?" His merry eyes take her in.

"I was just thinking . . ." She'll never know if Corey lives or dies.

"What's fizzing in that beautiful head?"

"I told Corey why it was wrong to fight the war. But he's probably going to fight anyway."

"Therefore he knows more than the next guy in the unit. He's really cannon fodder if he doesn't have a handle on what's going on. Hey, you did what you could, so . . . put your worries away." He mimes holding a microphone as if to sing.

"No singing allowed."

"Of course not, my little Stalinist."

"Shut up. I am not."

"Okay, but a minor rigidity keeps that posture straight. And you sure do not take anything lightly." He inhales a toke deeply, which makes a slight hissing sound.

"Why should I?"

"Fun? How about that, Josie?"

"If I wanted fun, I'd do other things."

"Like?" He straddles a chair, his expression eager.

"Travel, see a thousand flicks, spend hours reading novels. None of which there's time to do now." She certainly wouldn't choose to sleep in a windowless back room filled with boxes and musty smells.

"Wrong answer, muffin. The movement is about bringing sunshine into the misery of daily existence. Why else do this?"

"Because racism and body bags are . . ."

"That's the point, Josie. Everything is rotten in Empireland, and the movement needs to be an example of why it's worth fighting to change it."

His playful expression, that go-easy attitude, implying it'll all work out in the end—it scares her.

"Got you speechless, did I? Here, take a drag." His eyes

steady on her, he places the joint in her mouth. His fingers brush her lips. Thin smoke curls up between them. She inhales the sweet taste, lets the smoke rest inside her before exhaling.

"I don't see things the way you do, Ben. So much that's bad needs to change; trying to turn it all around is serious business. How can anyone feel easy about that?"

"Ah, good woman, you've made my point. If we're going to spend the next many years revolutionizing a society already so uptight the Puritans would feel right at home, we'd better take some pleasure doing so."

"Doesn't it excite you to be a part of making history?"

"Absolutely."

"Wouldn't it be great if someday the workers who want their salaries but hate their jobs would be able to get satisfaction from both?"

"Of course."

Unlike her father, he's never been stuck in a job where the day never seems to end. He grew up in a family that gave him a sense of entitlement she can barely imagine. Still, he's always ready to do the most unglamorous work with a smile.

"Why did you stay here tonight?"

"To protect you," he teases, throwing up his arms to cover his face.

"Well, thanks, mister, but I do fine on my own."

"Actually, we haven't hung out recently."

"In case you didn't notice, this place has turned into a full-time event, plus there's my job."

"I notice everything, sweet pea; don't you ever think otherwise. Your big eyes, your curly caramel locks, the bubbly energy in your petite body, the—"

"Enough, Ben."

"Let's creep into one sleeping bag."

"No thanks."

"What's the problem?" His tone slightly pleading.

"You know what'll happen, and I'm not interested."

"Oh, monogamy shit. Do you think Melvin shares your philosophy?"

"Why do you say that? If you know something I don't—"

"Whoa there, I'm surmising, that's all."

"Shit, Ben. Take your ego for a walk, will you?"

She begins to pick up trash, remembers she has to call Melvin. She does. No one answers. He doesn't like her to call him at the Panther office and give the feds more information about his private life.

Ben sweeps the floor, then begins emptying the ashtrays. Busy at their chores, neither one says anything for a while. When they're done, she turns off the front room lights, and they retire to the back room. Ben climbs into the spare sleeping bag, arms crossed beneath his head, burning roach dying in the ashtray, which she empties down the toilet. She tightens the sheet on the cot, lifts the blanket off a shelf, then switches off the back room lights. A shaft of moonlight opens across the floor.

"Are you angry?" he asks.

"No."

"It would really upset me."

"I'm not, Ben. Go to sleep."

"Resentment's like a cesspool."

"Friends forever, honestly." She stretches out, feeling each vertebra hit the thin mattress. Corey's face floats into her head. There's so much about people she doesn't know. Maybe someday she will travel. Isn't it one of the best ways to learn about life elsewhere? It's strange to think that her parents crossed the ocean and she hasn't even been to North Dakota. That may not be the first place she'd want to visit, but—

Shattering glass explodes the silence. In a blank instant of disbelief, she grabs on to each side of the cot. Something hard whacks against wood. A bomb? A rock? Ben is pushing her off the cot onto the floor while one arm shields his head. She wants to say it's coming from out front, but fear has her by the throat. Suddenly, there's a loud gush of liquid. Water pipe? The coffee urn? More glass shatters. The mirrors? Seven years bad luck if they live. Loud pings like chunks of hail on a car top. Rubber bullets? Buckshot?

Ben whispers, "I don't think it's the cops . . . not their style. I'm going to see what's what, then call the police."

"No, don't. You can't call the police."

"I'm not about to let those fascist pigs, whoever they are, get away with this," he whispers frantically.

She grabs his arm. "Stuff is hidden in the cellar. I don't know what. I don't know where. The police will search. You can't call them." Her words quick and breathless.

He stares at her. "I'm going out there. We need people. I'm phoning Lowell." Down on all fours he begins to crawl out of the back room.

Shots continue to ping off surfaces. Suddenly the moonlight is frightening.

Any minute someone will step through the shattered glass to enter the back room. Terror dries her mouth. She can't cry out, can't run; she's trapped in a horror show.

"Shit!" Ben's voice rises in a wail.

Afraid to move, afraid not to, afraid to find out what happened, afraid to stay here alone, she crawls out to find Ben lying flat on his back.

"Switch on the lights," he whispers urgently.

"Are you crazy?" she whispers back.

"The lights. They think no one's here. It's the only way they might stop." His voice raspy.

With racing heart and a prayer for help to a God she never consults, she sidles along the never-ending wall, her fingers searching for the light switch. The fluorescents flicker on, looking like an eerie evening sun. She doesn't move. The shooting stops as suddenly as it began.

The floor is covered with pieces of glass and mutilated poster faces, a nose there, a cheek here, a horrid singing mouth. She carefully weaves between shards of glass, then clears a space to kneel beside Ben." His thigh is bleeding through the denim of his jeans.

"Josie?"

"I'm here."

"I'm so cold."

His weak voice frightens her. What to do? He needs a hospital. The Vietnamese wouldn't leave a comrade in a pool of blood.

"Be right back." She grabs a quarter, dials for an ambulance, then brings out the blanket and covers his trembling body. No doubt the police will show up along with the ambulance. Whatever the consequences, Ben has to be taken care of. She leans close, takes his icy hand. "They'll disinfect the wound, give you some antibiotics, some groovy painkillers; you'll be fine. When you wake up, it'll be a great story. Ben, can you hear me?" She strokes his clammy forehead, bristly cheek, ignores the blood seeping out from under the blanket, and continues to talk to him softly, her words filled with make-believe certainty, until the ambulance siren is at its loudest.

"The ER will take good care of you. I'll phone our friends and wait here to be picked up."

The ambulance guys are gentle. They work quickly, slip a tourniquet around Ben's thigh, and lift him onto a stretcher. Was it buckshot? She's afraid to ask.

"Are you all right, miss?" A policeman and his partner appear in the doorway.

"Yes, my friends are coming to take me home." Once again, she prays, Dear God of good people, keep them out of the cellar. The policemen walk through to investigate the damage. They enter the back room, where the door to the cellar is located. She craves Melvin's presence with a hunger that cramps her belly but won't phone him, won't phone anyone yet. If they do find the carton, it'll be her and maybe Ben who will have to answer for it. Bad enough. Of course, she'll deny knowing anything.

After what feels like a million years but is only a few minutes, she follows the policemen outside. The ambulance has taken off. They write down her name, but instead of her address, she gives them Johnny's address. Might as well provide some grist for his paranoia. She answers a few more questions of no importance and promises to be at the town precinct the next day to make a report. As the police get into their car and pull away, she can't help thinking that Johnny would've been more thorough in his search.

It's too dark to see the adjacent rocky embankment, but she wonders if the shooters are still out there. Wrapping her arms around her torso for more than warmth, she turns to take in the almost-complete destruction of the storefront.

Dawn is breaking by the time Nina drops her off at her apartment. Melvin hugs her hard, says, "Thank God you're okay, sweet girl. Lowell phoned from the hospital. Ben isn't hurt bad, just freaked." Then he whispers, "The carton didn't get there yet."

The rising sun, as bright as cooked peaches, streams through the window, but it won't stop her from sleeping.

A loud noise wakes her. It's thunder. Lightening shocks the room. Rain pelts the windows. Yesterday comes rushing back. How long has she slept? Melvin, already dressed, is fiddling in the kitchen. He must've gotten up late. Maybe she'll close her eyes again, reach for sleep. "Hello." Unbidden, the word speaks itself.

"Coffee and cereal? Say yes; it's all we have."

"Yes." Rolling slowly out of bed, her body aches as if she's been carrying weights up and down steps.

Melvin places two cups of coffee on the table and sits beside her. She tips some dry cereal into a bowl, pours in milk. "I feel weird," she tells him.

"Of course."

"Of course?"

"Was that the first time you thought you were going to die . . ."

"I don't know . . . Yes . . ."

"At least you reached a ripe age without the thought."

"What?"

"Since I was a kid, I've wondered if my demise was close. Still do . . ."

"That's so freaking sad." He won't let her console him, but she tries anyway.

"Yeah, well . . . better to . . . Listen, about Christmas . . . I've been trying to convince my mom to visit us for the holiday. She doesn't like to travel and hasn't said yes. But if she does come, can she stay with us?"

"Yes, of course." She's only spoken to the woman on the phone. Having her visit, well . . . it makes Josie nervous. Melvin told her long ago that his mother worries about his being with a white woman. His father died when he was a baby, but he's close to his mother. If his mother does visit, she'll prove that she's the best girlfriend Melvin could have. "It'll be great to have her here."

"Excellent."

On Christmas Day, her family gathers at Celia's house. She didn't join them last holiday, wouldn't go without Melvin and wouldn't expose him to their racism. It's not his job to help them deal with it. But it saddens her that she can't share him the way that Celia shared Paul or Johnny does Terry. Even Richie would sometimes bring his girlfriend of the month to meet everyone. When Richie returns, she and Melvin will spend lots of time with him. They'll introduce Richie to their favorite bar. Maybe he'll stay over now and then.

"I'm off to the office, then a bunch of meetings and so forth. Miles did a stint serving breakfast one morning a few weeks ago. He didn't talk much, seemed preoccupied."

"He is, but he won't let on why. Listen, with the coffeehouse destroyed, I'm free to put in some time before work at the breakfast program."

"Okay, are you considering going to make that report today?"

"No way. No way."

"Right. Good. But you need to stay home. Call in sick. Today you need to get over yesterday."

"I'm over it."

"No you're not." He grabs his leather jacket. "See you later."

The rain darkens the apartment, adding to her gloomy mood. She could switch on more lights but doesn't. She isn't hungry and pushes aside the cereal. Last night seems surreal. Visiting the scene in her head causes some of the terror to return. Did she actually believe she'd die? She isn't sure, but the possibility of great harm seemed near. Her mother doesn't revisit disasters that have passed. Doing so is considered a waste of time. It happened. It can't be changed. The dictum is "No pussyfooting, hand-holding, namby-pamby; move on."

Friends will soon phone, curious to know everything about the coffeehouse attack. What is there to tell? Whoever they were, they came, shot up the place, and then disappeared. And how is she doing? Fine, a little buzzed out but fine. How else to explain the aftershock of the attack? She hasn't the words and doesn't want to delve. So, fine is what she'll say. Except to Ben, who will want to commiserate after he's released from the hospital.

13

Celia walks east on crowded Fifty-Seventh Street, where clusters of people rush out of office buildings and disperse in every direction. The ebb and flow of so much people traffic makes her feel vulnerable. It's as if the density will somehow devour her.

Her short jacket, chosen carefully for tonight, does little to keep her warm. She eyed the long Indian scarf that Paul bought her but chose to go without it. Though it's been a while, anything to do with Paul still hurts. For months before he took off, there were no gigs; he was at home and high most of the time. Did he even know she was watching?

Telling her sons about his departure was painful. She said his addiction was an illness and that he didn't want to burden them with his care. Miles and Sam had nothing to say. Quince still hasn't written back. With her sons off busy doing their thing, the house is empty most of the time. To be no longer needed by them in the same ways is an adjustment.

She hopes the bar Denise chose won't be packed three deep. She could've decided to stay home comfortable, watch TV, read a book, or something. Instead, she let her friend convince her. For days, Denise has been pestering her to go out and have some fun. Insisting that it's time, that if she doesn't, she'll end up as dry as a leaf in winter, that she's young, that she's ready. Though what ready is supposed to feel like is beyond her.

Denise waits inside the hotel bar dressed in a black sheath and high-heel pumps. She looks daring, inviting, and a bit scary.

The wood-paneled decor is elegant. Voices are low and laughter discreet, the barstools occupied by well-dressed men and women. Nothing here is anything like the dives she and Paul frequented.

They sit at a small round table. The waiter arrives and they order two Martinis with extra olives.

"It's awfully quiet for a bar," Denise says.

"It's respectful. That's nice too."

"Maybe too polite for anyone to come over and say hello," Denise says.

"You don't know that."

The waiter places the drinks on the table and leaves without a word.

"Bet you a second Martini. Look around. Most of the men are here with women."

"It's okay, Denise. We'll get a little high, tell each other funny stories. What's wrong with that?"

"Here's a funny story. Adele's husband, a man who comes and goes with the tides, arrived home drunk after another week away to no one knows where. He's ashamed and becomes a doting husband. Does she throw him out? No. Why? She enjoys his guilt and is letting her girls get their fill of him. As soon as his shame evaporates, she's telling him to get out for good."

"That's not funny."

"You don't have the proper sense of humor."

"Which is what?"

"Who takes care of the house? Who takes care of the kids? Who worries about doctors' visits, food in the fridge, children's social lives? Not them, us. We think we can't live without them, but actually we already do. That's the joke. And here's the funniest part: We aren't aware of any of this when we're really young, because we want love, children, and companionship. We get the children."

"Stop, Denise. You're making me cry."

"Yeah, well, I always get my audience wrong."

"Do you think Adele will really do it?"

"No. Do I think her husband will fuck around again? Yes. Will I say so? No. You know why? Because she'll blame me—not him—for hurting her. How's that for ridiculous?"

"Your cynicism is charming," she says.

"Do you think I've been on an island since Sal left? Nine out of the ten men who ask me out are married."

"How's your daughter?" She doesn't want to discuss men leaving.

"That's one way to change the subject. Fine. She graduates high school in June. How does Miles like college?"

"He's so involved with everything around the war I only pray he doesn't fail his subjects and get drafted."

"These young people dressed like winos, prancing around, drugged up, it's disgusting."

She flashes on Josie, who, like Miles, is entirely taken up with politics. "Not all of them. They hate the war. I don't love it either."

"What's to love? But the way these hippie-dippie kids carry on, you'd think life was happening for the first time and only to them."

"You're jealous because the young women look good in those awful boots."

"True. And the beards, on the men that is. I can't even stand a day's growth. Can you imagine ten inches around the chin? It would be like sleeping with an animal."

She laughs. "Paul's the only man I ever slept with."

Denise raises her dark brows. "It's time to break the spell. At first you won't feel a thing, then it gets better, I promise."

It won't get better, she doesn't say. Emptiness can't be filled willy-nilly. But why argue?

"Let's pool some cash, grab a cab to Tic Tack Inn. It's close to home, and we can dance there. It'll cheer you. I bet the men will fight to pay for our drinks. Get us out of this funeral parlor."

February something

Josie, my sister, what a place this is, but I'll put off
inviting you for a visit, although you do keep bothering
me for details. Thing is, one day slides into the next, and
if there's a difference, it disappears like we do. How can
everything that happens happen and still stay the same?
It's deranging. Even when we set up another base—a
joke and a half—it looks and feels like yesterday. So I
wonder if I've actually moved anywhere. Once I tied a
piece of material around a tree trunk so I'd know if I
returned there. I never found it, no surprise. Besides, trees
are everywhere, green, green, green, everything green.
Remember the coloring books Ma bought us? We'd fill in
the pages until there was no white space left. Here, too,
foliage chokes the air, can't see a fucking thing.

Yes to your slogan. Bring the troops home right now.
However, no piece-of-shit brass will agree. Please, don't
send posters or articles. The guys would be too insulted.
No picture or article is going to tell us anything we don't
already breathe firsthand. By the way (and don't adver-
tise this) no one gets through a day or night here with-
out major assistance. My present aid (think high) is al-
mond-toasted hash, next best thing to black beauties, and
here's the trade-off: for every life on the line, there's a stash
of excellent drugs provided.

A few nights ago out on patrol, my buddy and I shared
a weed of such sweet taste and smell it must have grown
in heaven. We cupped the tip so none of the birds in the
trees, who have better than 20/20 vision and hearing you

wouldn't believe, would relate to us. There I was drifting in and out of reverie, moon close enough to touch (which is scary), and Uncle Lou floats into my head. And I'm thinking about Easter dinner when he's telling us about his job at the Ford plant, how the speedup was so great he could only manage to tighten every other bolt. And suddenly this feels hilarious. I can't control myself. Stuff my fist in my mouth and laughter spurts past it. I'm going to die laughing. Can't stop, Josie. Every other bolt (outrageous, I know) is so fucking funny I'm passing out with mirth, laughter filling my gut. I go belly down, press my mouth into the dirt but the laughter explodes, oh God, it felt so good, hurt so much keeping it in. Story ends this way: woke up the neighbors in the trees, who began shooting. My buddy lost his eye. That's a day in the life . . . every event a lesson in what you better not ever do again in this fucked-up place, so no more laughing. Thing is, nothing, absolutely nothing, makes sense here. The only reason to kill the little bastards is to save my ass and those of my buddies, who look out for mine. Otherwise who are these people? Everyone looks like everyone else, and what does a Communist look like anyway? It feels like such a waste.

You can't really want to read this stuff, but what else can I write about? Ah yes, the medals, they're a trip and a half. Kill more than three, you get a medal. Lose a leg, get a medal. Get shot saving your buddy, get a medal. Who's crazy enough to want a medal? One thing for sure, the distance between here and home gets longer, wider, and more complicated by the hour. In a way, that's okay, even helpful.

Received Celia's letter about Paul. Poor guy, right? I mean, I always liked him. Do you think she's looking for him? I wonder how much West Point will change Quince. He may actually end up in this forsaken place when he graduates. As the guys here say, no end in sight except one's own. Terry wrote me that Ma's volunteering two hours a day in the church on Tremont. Hope she's not cleaning it, for God's sake. At the end of T's letter, Johnny noted he's putting in more overtime than ever because of you antiwar guys. Now, there's someone who'd relate to Nam. I mean, how often does he get a chance to shoot his weapon in the Bronx?

Yes, of course I've heard about the Black Panthers. They're legend here. Several black guys in my unit came back from R&R with Panther tattoos. Melvin sounds like one tough dude, but then again, from everything you've said, he doesn't really. I plan to meet the man someday.

So what's next in your obstacle course? You didn't say. I'll write when I can, but don't get nervous if I can't.

Love you kid,
Richie

-14-

The rally is over. People cluster around Melvin to congratulate him. Her admiration will be bestowed at home tonight. His speech defending the Panther 21 and excoriating the police for false arrest was electric, the tone dynamic. Thank the universe he wasn't one of those arrested, though he seems almost disappointed. Maybe he thinks it means that he's not as important. Anyway, he's working around the clock to raise money for his comrades' defense.

The police are out in force, some on horses. As usual she searches their numbers for Johnny; so far, so good, no Johnny. Anyway, what could he do? Pull her out of the crowd? That would be unprofessional. If he's anything, he's respectful of every rule that attends to his position. God, why in heaven's name is Johnny taking up residence in her head? Her family manages to spook her even when they're nowhere to be seen.

She's reluctant to leave, but Maisie is waiting. She heads to Central Park, already sorry she didn't stay to chat with some of the Panthers, especially Rosemary. After working at the breakfast program last week, the two of them spent quality time together. A lot of personal insights were shared. Rosemary, who was born and raised in Harlem, intends one day to become a physical therapist. Josie shared how glad she was to get away from her suffocating family, their values, and the South Bronx. No, she admitted, she had no idea what she wanted to become when all the shit was behind them. Later that day, thinking about Rosemary, she wondered if not having a particular career in mind was a result of her having dropped out of high school or of a belief that the movement, with all of its needs and activities, would last through her lifetime. Definitely something to ponder.

The tall buildings bordering Central Park are golden in the soon-to-vanish sun. An elderly man on a bench turns his face to catch the last rays. Children climbing nearby rocks call loudly to one another.

Sitting cross-legged beneath a chestnut tree, Maisie waves to her. Josie joins her on the softening ground.

"I have serious a conversation to share," Maisie greets her.

"Okay."

"We need to leave the male-dominated movement and form a separate women's organization to develop our own politics. Women are already doing that elsewhere."

"We have a women's caucus."

"Not good enough," Maisie asserts. "Women want change. They-slash-we no longer want to spend more time at the mimeograph than in formulating theory. Do you have a problem with that?"

"Look, I just came from an intense rally. Melvin was riveting. The words are still creating noise in my head."

"You make my point."

She feels a spark of anger, but this is Maisie, her friend. "I don't understand."

"Instead of hearing me all you can focus on is what happened at a male-dominated rally, important as I'm sure it was. I'm asking: Do you have a problem with a separate movement?"

She doesn't appreciate being put on the spot. "Separating would dissipate too much energy. A lot is happening now. The struggle is changing, becoming more militant. People are writing manifestos on guerrilla warfare. Men are refusing to fight, disappearing to Canada or going to jail. It's the wrong time to create more havoc."

"We can be as antiracist and anti-imperialist as any man and still put forward women's issues. None of the male-dominated organizations will do both. Women's demands are seen as divisive or as later for that."

She isn't used to Maisie being so determined; it annoys her. "Perhaps at a future date," she says, unwilling to engage in a long-winded argument, anxious to get home.

"That's what women always say. Not the right time to leave, not the right time to change, not the right time to seize the time. It is, Josie. It's the perfect time."

"It would be a breach, though, don't you think?"

"What you're really saying is that movement men will be angry and rejecting. Who cares? Think about this. Why isn't it a breach to always have our politics explicated by men? Who are we in this movement? We sure as hell do as much, but the power remains theirs. And worse, they don't even recognize our oppression. They're mired in chauvinism." Maisie's eyes steady on her.

"Movement men aren't our enemies. Think Nixon—"

"If you define 'enemy' that way, of course. But if you define 'enemy' as any man who keeps us from our liberation, then too many movement men do just that."

She feels gut checked, accused of something she didn't do, judged for something she doesn't feel. Actually, men often gut check: make harsh statements about people's politics. She hates that. But saying so would just prolong the discussion. "Have you shared your thoughts with Nina?"

"Nina believes we can raise women's consciousness within the same organization as men. But since they moved in together, she's influenced by Lowell. He'd be totally pissed at the idea. What about Melvin?"

"We do our own things. What matters are the goals. He might think it stupid to pull out of a growing movement just now. He already believes white radicals aren't committed enough. Anyway, I'm not convinced a separate women's movement is worth the disruption." Though she does believe that disruption is good. It moves things, lets you see what might be hidden beneath. Isn't that what she tells everyone?

"I've been discussing my hopes, dreams, and despair as well as my politics with a group of women. It's a wonderful experience to find others who understand the way I feel. Women energize each other because deep down we each know the truth about our lives. Sharing feelings is more than cleansing; it's revolutionary. Think about this: How comfortable would you be talking about the lack of good birth control with Lowell in the room? Would men write a flyer calling for an end to the bombing on one side and an end to women's oppression on the other? Only a separate women's movement can make that happen." Maisie's voice loud with certainty.

"I'm not saying you're wrong, just that it doesn't seem feasible now."

"It's already happening, Josie. Women are beginning to view the world through our own experiences. The political will become personal and that's powerful. We're not there yet, but the dogs are waking. Anyway, my group is planning a women's sit-in at a radio news station. We intend to read a declaration of women's demands over the air."

"What about an end to the war, racism?"

"They are also our demands. We're calling ourselves the Mother Jones Brigade."

"Why not the Madame Binh Brigade?"

"Why not? Come to the planning meeting; bring it up."

Melvin will dig the action. Why for one fucking second should that matter?

On Josie's way to the supermarket, Maisie's words refuse to let go. She should've been more encouraging. Why wasn't she? The word "separate" frightens her. It brings to mind Melvin's Blackness and her whiteness. It signifies aloneness or maybe even abandonment, but of whom? The men? Melvin? No, that can't be.

In the brightly lit supermarket, which is in stark contrast to the falling darkness, she does her best to shunt Maisie's words aside. She'll buy a box of linguine and a jar of spaghetti sauce and then pick up a bottle of cheap red. They'll toast Melvin's success at the rally. She isn't sure when he'll arrive home, but he did say he'd see her at dinner.

She grabs her items, then waits impatiently to pay. The line is long. In front of her, a woman's cart is filled with jars of baby food.

"It must be expensive having a baby these days," Josie says.

"If I didn't have to work, I'd make this shit myself. A few vegetables and a strainer, but who has time?" The woman's tired voice, tired face, and slumped shoulders underscore her words.

"We should be grateful for supermarkets, I guess."

"Yeah, well . . . save time but spend too much money." The woman shakes her head.

Would this woman give a fuck about a separate women's movement? How would it benefit her? Or is a separate movement only for the already enlightened? She should've asked Maisie *that*. Obviously she's still somewhat pissed at her friend. She doesn't like being blindsided, especially if the idea has merit.

She sets out two bowls, two glasses for wine. The pasta water has begun to boil. The phone rings. Oh, please, no, she thinks, turning off the flame.

"Hello."

"Baby, something's come up. I'll be home in a few hours or less. Tell you about why later."

"I just cooked us dinner, wine and all. To celebrate. It was a great speech, Melvin."

"Sorry a million times over, really have to do this. I'll hurry."

Jesus. What now? she worries. "Are you okay?"

"Couldn't be better. Save me some of the wine."

"That depends."

She could eat and then do a little cleanup of the apartment, which smells as if the pile of dirty clothing in the corner has come alive. Even if Maisie's right, is it the—

There's a hard, rapid knocking at the door.

No one she knows would bang like that. She doesn't respond. The knocking persists as if the person knows she's right there.

"It's Johnny. Let me in."

Damn. She unlocks the door, prays Melvin doesn't get home while Johnny's here.

In uniform he appears taller, broader. He's never visited before. Seeing things through his eyes, she notes the Panther newspapers and radical magazines strewn everywhere, also the political posters that paper the walls.

"How dare you give my address to the New Jersey police for your slimy business? Who do you think you are, queen of crap?" Blue eyes blazing, he tosses his cap on the table.

"Sorry, it was a nervous moment. I'll call and correct it. I'm about to leave now."

"Too easy, Josephine Anna Marie Russo, too easy by far. You're a little snot, never calling Ma."

"Who made you family guardian?"

"Who else is there? And you bringing shame on your family, engaging in dangerous activities, leading Miles down the alley with you. Don't you care?"

He always had a temper but never at her, his little sister.

"Don't think I'm stupid," he says.

"Why would I think that?"

"Because you believe you're better than the rest of us ordinary people. Who are the longhair guys you mess with? No one you can bring home, that's for sure. You think you can fight city hall and win. You can't. It's a waste of your time. Sooner than later you'll be caught doing something illegal. You'll be jailed, maybe killed, kill Ma too. A coffeehouse? Giving soldiers treasonous information? I've been in law enforcement enough years to know that you'll pay dearly."

He's circling her, taking in the environs, looking for what she isn't sure.

"Fighting the police with sticks and stones, how dumb is that? Are you looking for broken bones? None of your friends show any respect. They even dress dirty. What kind of a person spits at officers, calls us pigs? Who treats authority like that?"

He continues to roam the apartment, lifting, touching, his eyes a camera. What gives him the right? This is her home. "You should go. Now."

"I haven't finished yet."

"I think you have." She tells herself that Melvin only just phoned; he couldn't possibly be on the way home.

"So you've become like the rest of them, disrespecting family, authority? If Pa was still alive, he'd have another heart attack."

How dare he invoke her father? "You think you're authority? They stick a gun in your pants, a pair of handcuffs on your ass, and guess what? Your so-called authority is most useful to rich people who need you to clean up and do the dirty work. You're hired to help the Man keep his property private. You're hired to protect them, not you and yours. The department gives you a steady paycheck to shut you up and keep you where they need you to be. They buy your allegiance, and you think it's your choice. You'll retire early and wonder why you're depressed for the rest of your life. What really upsets you is seeing my friends go after real values, real hope, real freedom and treat you like you're just in the way, which you are." Near tears, she stops.

He looks at her but says nothing. That he isn't responding upsets her.

"Where's Miles?" he asks.

"What?"

"Celia said he never picked up his draft notice." His tone subdued.

"Celia wants him to go in the army?"

"She doesn't want him in jail."

"I haven't seen him in weeks."

"I don't believe you."

"Tell me something: If you find Miles, are you going to turn him in?"

"Don't be stupid. I want to make him think about his choices. He's a college guy, smart, could go places, but with a criminal record, he'll end up worse than his father. Celia thought you'd help; she knows how close you two are."

Not for a second does she believe Celia sent him. "I don't know where he is, but I do know he'd rather go to jail than fight in this war."

"He can't escape the law, Josie. That's a fact."

"Going to jail could save his life. Richie is already in the war. How many sacrifices do you need?"

"I just want to talk to him." He crosses both hands in front of his belly, but he's not at ease.

"If Miles contacts me, I'll give him your message," she says.

He picks up his cap. "And call Ma. Are you listening?" He opens the door, but not before taking note of the three locks, then closes it softly.

He registered every piece of paper in the apartment, of that she's certain. He's smart, tough, and relentless, like her.

-15-

She walks quickly uptown. Broadway stretches awake beneath the humid June morning. It's early. Many stores still shuttered. Well-stocked outdoor fruit stands offer an occasional passerby with a quick hand a free apple. No one steals for fun, she's heard herself say many times, but lately it seems some do. Not just apples.

Still rankled by Johnny's visit yesterday, she couldn't settle. It wasn't so much what he said, which was bullshit, but the angry words with which she responded that still upset her. They must've been hurtful. He is her brother. It was the worst day for him to show up. Maisie's suggestion was batting at her brain, and she was nervous that Melvin could somehow arrive home at any moment. Her worry was wasted. He didn't come home at all. He phoned around midnight, said they should meet today for breakfast at their coffee shop. He wouldn't say anything more, and she knew not to probe.

After his call her mind refused to quiet. The questions wouldn't abate. Was Melvin about to tell her that he has to disappear, go underground like others in the movement have already done? If so, could she go with him? They would need money, which they don't have. Where would they get it? Where would they hide? Would he choose to immerse himself in a Black neighborhood where she'd stick out like a sore thumb? Oh lord, it all made her feel so powerless.

Melvin is in a booth when she arrives at the coffee shop. They touch fingers across the table. The steam-fogged windows offer coziness; the smells of bacon and fried eggs rise with the greasy smoke. There's a scattering of people at tables, mostly Columbia University students. One overworked, overweight waiter trundles back and forth with orders.

"I ordered for both of us," he says.

"Missed you at home last night."

"Me too," he says, without conviction, though it's clear he's excited.

"So . . . tell . . ." she prompts, trying not to sound as alarmed as she feels.

He leans forward as if to pick something out of her hair and whispers. "It's going to happen. Not sure for how long. Mexico, Cuba, then Ghana."

"You have to disappear?"

"Not at all. I'm being sent as an emissary of the Panthers to open international offices. We want to expand. It's the right time."

She wants to go with him, not only to be with him, but also to visit those countries. But who would send her? Not the Panthers. Not her family. Maybe Nina's wealthy father, she thinks bitterly.

"Who's paying?" she asks.

"Some rich dudes."

"Why not use the money for the Panther bail fund?" Her voice as low as his.

"Good question. We rolled the idea back and forth for hours

last night and decided progressing to international stature is more important. A presence in the world strengthens the party here. Look at Malcolm; he knew when to travel."

Malcolm was murdered, she doesn't say. "I could worry a lot."

"Josie, if you want to worry your ass, worry twenty-four a day while I'm here, because no one there is gunning for us, okay? The police filling Black Panthers with bullets could happen only in the US."

When he talks like this, like now, she needs to peel away the layers, find the heart of the matter, which is what, she can't say. She nods, though, because they're in a public place, and everything they utter must be circumspect.

"I'll drop by the apartment this afternoon to pack a few things. Look, I'll miss you hard," he adds.

She nods, too close to tears to utter a word.

The waiter sets down their English muffins and coffee and stands for a moment as if wanting to make sure they eat, or is it that they're the only Black and white couple in the restaurant?

They walk briskly toward the subway station. She can't help but notice his elation and is careful not to rain on his parade. But the warmth of their daily lives feels upended.

"I'll try and call you. The feds will know where I am as soon as I land, so what the hell? Just don't complicate the conversation, understand?" It's a warning to be brief and trite, and something in her wants to say, Why not send a postcard? Except hearing his voice will reassure her. Some women kiss their men good-bye, knowing they'll return at six. Some women bid farewell at airports with their itineraries in hand, and some watch prison gates close, but they can visit. She, too, needs something to grasp while his body is gone and his soul invested elsewhere. But what that could be, she has no idea.

Outside the subway entrance, him going uptown to the Panther office, her downtown to work, they stand close enough for her to breathe in his tea-like scent. His wispy beard a bit longer now, his bush of hair modified by an inch or two, the shine in his eyes as bright as ever. Yet a Black man and a white woman who don't crave attention kissing passionately in the middle of the street isn't going to happen. Instead she lightly brushes his lips with her own and for the first time this morning feels him focus on her. Anywhere else and they'd be locked together. His hand tightens around her arm, and he whispers, "I'm scarred from our love, baby, and plan never to heal. I'm already looking forward to homecoming." He slides something into her pocket. "Rosemary's private pay phone. Don't speak to anyone else. It's for emergencies only, not the simple cold, but on a scale of lung cancer. And, baby, memorize the number." His finger travels across her cheek, and for a moment he gazes at her. "You take care, okay?"

Watching him disappear down the subway steps, she wants to call out, Take me with you; I'll be good. A child's cry ahead of abandonment.

-16-

The Bronx bar is familiar. A TV drones on about nothing that could faintly interest her. Several men on barstools glance at her, then return their eyes to the screen. The afternoon light barely reaches into the rear, where music throbs just above low. It's Saturday and Celia phoned her too early this morning and insisted they meet but wouldn't say why.

Whenever the phone rings, she prays it will be Melvin, but it's been two weeks without a word. She tries to convince herself that her sadness is simply due to missing him but hasn't quite succeeded. Her worries, though, are crystal clear. What if he's hurt or has been arrested or is under some other duress? Who would contact her? What if something—she has no idea what—stops him from returning? The unanswerable questions follow her like the tail of a kite. She could phone Rosemary to ask if all's well but, even as she thinks this, knows she won't dial that number just to be reassured. Though she's filled her evenings and weekends with even more activity, Melvin is never far from her thoughts.

Celia sits at a back table nursing a glass of white wine.

As Josie is about to settle into a chair, Celia captures her wrist. "Miles is my son. I won't be shut out. You can't know anything I don't know, understand? The boy is gone, snatched away, living or not living with people I've never met, but

122

hidden from me. I won't stand for it, Josie. He's mine. I have a right to him. I won't leave here without information. You're my only link. Look at me. I can't eat, can't sleep; he's in my head wherever I am. I can't live this way. I don't give a shit about the army. I don't care if he's in Canada, but I must know how to reach him. He's my breath, my firstborn. No one can keep my son from me, not you or anyone." Her expression intense, eyes brimming, fingers cold.

"I don't know where he is now. That's the truth. He might phone me at work to set up a visit. If he does, I'll insist he see you. I swear." She, too, has been worried about Miles. And has tried to reach him through friends and potential conduits, but no luck.

"Tell him that I won't try to change his mind, that I'll support his choice not to go into the army. But that he must contact me."

"I hear you. I will." And she offers a quick prayer that Miles will contact her. However, talking about him in this place makes her nervous. The bar is a hangout for cops, firemen, and others who favor uniforms.

Her sister pushes back her chair. "I'm getting a refill. What do you want?"

"A beer, any kind." Her sturdy sister's desperation is more than upsetting; it's disorienting. It saddens her to see Celia so vulnerable and close to hysteria. Celia's the sibling who is expected to and does show up at all family functions, the one for whom and from whom love flows without question or criticism. Josie will try harder to find a way to send Miles another message asking him to get in touch. Suddenly, a flame of anger heats her cheeks. Miles, Melvin, each doing their thing while she and Celia worry and suffer. It sucks.

"Thanks for coming up here. I couldn't face going into Manhattan." Celia pulls an envelope out of her pocket. "The draft notice, what should I do with it?"

"Nothing. It's not addressed to you. Leave it in his bedroom. He never picked it up."

"But I opened it."

"If anyone asks, you did so by mistake."

"Who's going to ask?"

"Maybe no one, or someone from Selective Service. There are thousands of men not responding to the draft. Miles isn't the most important one."

"What if he's roaming around with no money?"

"He has friends everywhere. Don't worry. It's a movement; people take care of each other."

"With what?"

"Some of us work. There's food, lodging, cigarettes, movies. We're organized."

"I hope that's true."

"I haven't been inside this bar in a long time." She needs to end talk about Miles. "I used to spend Saturday nights here with friends."

Those nights feel like part of another life, which they were. Filled with dumb conversations about things they wanted but didn't have, which, come to think of it, was a lot of things. Money was a big topic, how and where to get it, but no answers were offered. There was always a fair amount of whining about how come other people's lives were so much easier.

After a few beers, they'd move to another bar and have a few more beers until night descended into predawn. Then two couples to a car, they'd drive to the most littered sites of the Bronx, between the river and the rails or under the Whitestone Bridge, where they'd park and make out.

"I come here sometimes with Denise," Celia says.

"Oh?"

"Oh what?"

"Just to drink?" she asks.

"They have dancing on Friday nights. It's Denise; she's lonely, doesn't want to come here by herself."

"Have you danced with men?"

"Of course, even when Paul . . ."

"Yeah, right, even when Paul. Any word from him, anything?"

"Nope."

"It's good he went. It might've been worse if he'd stayed. You would've had to watch him get wasted."

"That's so harsh."

"It's you I'm thinking about, Celia."

"Yeah, okay. I don't want to talk about Paul. Do you plan to visit Ma while you're up here?"

"No. I have a meeting I need to attend." It's true. It's a run-through for the women's action. "I called Ma a few days ago. She isn't a talker, that's for sure."

"Not on the phone, I know. She seems to like living with Terry and Johnny, and I don't think she misses the restaurant either. The money from the sale was put into an account for whatever she needs."

"Johnny took care of everything?" she asks lightly.

"Is that a problem? Did you want to have a hand in it?"

"A little testy, aren't you?"

"I'm grateful. With Paul gone and now Miles, I certainly

didn't want to deal with Ma. Anyway, until you have children, you won't understand the misery when a child is in danger."

"Children aren't on my agenda." She hates these ridiculous conversations.

"We'll see."

"Right, everything's subject to change."

"But I'm curious, why not?"

"At some point they'll view me the way some of my friends view their parents. Besides, why bring babies into a society that still lacks peace and justice? So how's Terry?"

"She's lost a lot of weight. Some fertility drug. It nauseates her."

"She ought to go off it."

"I agree, but Johnny wants a baby."

"Then let him take the pills."

Celia smiles, which feels like a victory.

"Whoa, did you hear that!" A shout from the bartender turns their heads. He's pointing at the TV screen, the volume now loud. A draft board has been bombed.

A sense of irrevocability lands on her shoulders like a lead cape. It's done, finished, the commitment made, with no way out. Miles is stuck, glued to his decision, trapped in his life. No wonder he's been so out of touch. Maybe it isn't his collective. Except it is; she knows that. Of course she does. Poor Celia. What now? Stop, she orders her brain. Focus instead on the bartender's amazed voice, which has nothing to do with agreement but does contain surprise that someone had the balls to take on Goliath. Yes, that's what Miles would want her to hear. And think about the draft files destroyed. Imagine them tattered and scattered, all the general's men unable to fit them together again, thousands of young men's IDs lost to the draft. Isn't that something? Isn't that a good way to save lives? Isn't that a gift to families? But her throat feels dry, tight, her chest heavy, and she offers up a silent prayer that no one was hurt.

She glances at Celia, who seems oblivious to the import of the announcement. That Miles could have anything to do with the event would seem to her sister as ridiculous as an elephant drinking at the bar. Oh lord.

On her way home, Josie buys as many late-edition newspapers as she can get her hands on. In one, the collective's brief communiqué is reprinted. The communiqué takes responsibility for the bombing and goes on to explain the connection between destroying draft boards and ending the war. If she weren't already committed to stopping the war, would the explanation alter her thinking? She isn't sure. Does that mean she's not a true revolutionary? That she's allowing her emotions to interfere with political judgment?

A bunch of scenarios compete in her head: Miles hiding alone somewhere; Miles with friends, all of them congratulating one another on a successful action; Miles depressed; Miles elated. Was it loyalty to his collective that led him to this? Perhaps he disagreed but didn't want to break ranks or let them down. Desperation, maybe that's what it was: a sense that nothing is changing fast enough to make a difference. She's read about radicals in previous revolutions who have been led to commit such actions out of the pure terror of not knowing what else to do to effect change. But Miles is sensitive, kind, smart and many other good things; it bewilders her that he was a part of this. What she can't get her head around, what she doesn't want to believe, is the possibility that he had no qualms about the violence of the act.

17

A handful of flyers and a tightly folded banner are stuffed inside her shoulder bag. The day is warm, humid, and dreary. She's on her way to CBS, with Miles still heavy on her mind. Not having any information about him is sinking her.

She thinks that Lowell may be a source for news about Miles. But what if she's wrong? What if he doesn't realize it's Miles's collective that's responsible for the bombing? She has to risk him knowing, has no one else to ask for help. If a meeting is set up, what exactly does she want to say to Miles? Contact Celia, of course. She can't say, You shouldn't have done it. What were you thinking? She can't challenge him about something that's already been done. So what's the point of meeting? Maybe, like Celia, she just needs to see that he's okay. She remembers once watching a movie with Miles about a man who had to go into witness protection after testifying against a gangster. Discussing it later, Miles said if it was the right thing to do, he'd testify and then go into witness protection. She admitted it would be hard to leave everything she knew. Actually, though, she's done just that, hasn't she? Well . . . sort of.

She took today off as a personal day. But if she's arrested, her job at the hospital could be jeopardized. With Melvin bringing in only a miniscule salary, how to pay the rent would become problematic if she lost her job. Having little money doesn't scare her but having no money does. If she thinks about it, which she doesn't too often, she doesn't even know what she would do with a bundle of money. Having grown up in a home where money was never easily available, she doesn't sweat living paycheck to paycheck, except if there's no paycheck. It's complications like these that keep people from taking political action. Though she can't help but note that her movement friends aren't similarly challenged by such complications.

The CBS lobby is crowded. As planned, she joins the group of eleven women waiting at one of the elevator banks. On the seventeenth floor, the door slides open on a room with six gray metal desks divided by a center aisle. Three windows on one side of the room allow the grayish light to merge with the overhead fluorescents. Young to middle-aged women sit behind typewriters. At the front of the room is an office, the door ajar. Large calendars with schedules marked in black and red crayon cover cream-colored walls. Except for the rhythmic tapping that greets the ear, it's quiet, the secretaries intent on their work.

The women march down the center aisle. The typing ceases.

Nina unfurls her banner and says the words out loud. "Free our sisters; free ourselves. Power to the people."

Maisie, behind Nina, unfurls her banner and recites: "Black, brown, Asian, and white women work two shifts, get paid nothing for one and half the salary of men for the other."

Josie raises her banner and says: "Women hold up half the sky. We make a difference. End racism and bring the troops home now."

Before any of them have a chance to further explain their presence to the workers watching them, a tall man in his fifties with dark-framed glasses and close-cropped gray hair steps out of the back office. "Well, what do we have here?" he says playfully.

"This radio news station says nothing about women's oppression or racism and only repeats the government's lies about the war. We will not leave CBS until our demand to read a declaration of truth over the air is met." Nina sits down in the aisle.

"Women don't make the policies that send our men to war. Why should woman obey them? How many of the CBS bosses are women? How many of the reporters are women? How many people of color are in power? How often does a woman's signature appear on a paycheck?" Maisie and the rest of the women sit down.

"Okay, ladies, you've had your say; now it's time to leave." The man gestures as if to shoo them out. His condescending tone wraps itself around Josie's trachea.

Maisie stands and says, "We'll only speak to a woman reporter. We know you don't have many, but find one. We're not leaving here until you do."

The elevator door opens to release a CBS News reporter and a TV cameraman.

Returning to his office, the man shuts the door.

The women workers remain at their desks. The intruders remain seated on the floor.

Josie hands her banner to Maisie and begins to distribute flyers to the secretaries. "Even if you can't speak out here about racism, sexism, or the war for fear of losing your job, speak out somewhere against injustice and for peace."

A few uncomfortable, silent minutes follow before Marilyn James enters the room. Marilyn's cigarette-stained voice on the radio is familiar to countless people. Marilyn covers the bake sales, fairs, school picnics, runaway dogs, famous divorces, length of skirts, height of heels. But today is different. Today is political. Marilyn, in her forties, takes in the scene and without missing a blink asks Josie for a leaflet, which she reads silently. Then asks to take a look at the declaration. Nina hands her a copy. As Marilyn reads, there's no sound in the room.

"Okay," Marilyn says, "I'll do a brief intro. When I signal, one of you, come inside the booth and read your declaration."

℅   ℅   ℅

The evening sun still lingers as they head down to a new women's bar in the Village to celebrate. Tired from lack of sleep but feeling an unexpected and satisfying bond with the women, Josie can't imagine going straight home. For the first time in days, she's able to focus on the joy of success instead of on the plight of Miles, Melvin, or even Celia.

The bar is in the basement of a brownstone. Blue bulbs are strung across the ceiling like deflated balloons. Polka-dot-size tables circle the perimeter of the area, leaving space in the center to dance. White women sit at tables, drink at the bar, or dance to Joplin's electrifying voice. Melvin wouldn't be comfortable here. Would any man? she wonders. But Melvin would correctly point out that most of the women present are white.

Maisie orders two pitchers of beer. They push a few tables together, then gather round to assess the action and celebrate success. Josie's only half-listening, her eyes drawn to the three-quarter profile of a woman standing at the bar. After a minute or two of staring, she heads to the bar.

Gently touching the woman's arm, she's ready to say, Sorry, it's so dark in here, mistook you for . . . The woman turns to face her. One, two, three eternal seconds of gazing at each other before her cousin's arms seize her in a mad embrace.

They move apart to search each other's appearance. Grace's hair, no longer dark, is buttery yellow and buzz cut, with only a thin tail of braid reaching down endlessly. She sports a nose stud too. But her dark-chocolate eyes are a dead giveaway.

Grace tugs her a few feet toward another woman standing at the bar. "This is Carla, my lover; we live together in the Village." Grace's familiar voice dredges up a childhood of nightly secrets, but she never shared this one. How long did Grace know? It could be new or . . . Grace's eyes on her offer a warning: respond correctly or lose the prize.

"Carla, I'm so glad to meet you. I haven't seen my cousin for a long time, and I'm thrilled she's happy." Smiles all around.

Grace's arm wraps her waist. "So tell me, what's happening at home with everyone?"

Josie climbs the stairs to her apartment thinking about Grace, a chubby teen now a slim woman, the stencil of time leaving its marks. But also something else, something she can't get past, a veil of strangeness between them, like a spider web across an unused doorway. Apples off a similar tree, yes—their fathers were brothers—but landed far from each other. Grace kept referring to "home," no doubt her own as well as Josie's. But Josie's home is no longer on that Bronx street where she and Grace lived. Home is here, where she and Melvin live. How to fill in the missing years of growing up and growing apart?

Grace made her promise to conceal that she's a lesbian from

their two families. Sadly, she understands. Someday, but not yet, who you sleep with, love, live with, won't matter, or what's their struggle for?

She unlocks one, two, three locks, pushes hard on the door until she feels the police pole move.

"Baby mine, I've been waiting." He drapes a shawl around her shoulders, slides a thin silvery metal circle onto her middle finger, and pulls her toward the bed so she can view the cantaloupe-orange bedspread with its black zebra stripes.

"Melvin?" Barely a whisper.

"Come here, Josie; didn't mean to shock you. That there shawl's called a rebozo, and the ring, well, the ring is something special, one of a kind, made by the Vietnamese from a captured B-52 and given to me to give to you by Mr. Trinh. What do you think of that? And the bedspread—"

"When did you get back?" Her voice echoes from a distance.

"Last night. I spent it in Harlem debriefing. I've been here waiting for you and only you, sweet girl." His energy unnerving.

"You seem different. What is it? Your beard, it's gone. Is that it?"

"Difference can't be measured that way, but my experiences were life altering, details to follow."

To follow what, she doesn't need to wonder. Her mind is racing. Can she really bed down with him and make passionate love this minute, which he expects? "I found my cousin in a women's bar . . . She's a lesbian. She's in my life again. It's too strange. So amazing, finding her there, who'd ever think . . . ? I never expected, not now, maybe never, to see her again . . . I almost didn't recognize . . . And this morning we . . . women . . . took over CBS Radio station, TV cameras. The women were spectacular, and I . . ."

He places his hand over her mouth. "Calm, calm." His voice suddenly as familiar as the bones that sculpt his stern face.

"I'll take a shower."

"Don't want that, not at all, not a bit." His eyes two lit ponds. And it hits her like the proverbial bolt. He's here, in the flesh, intact, close enough to grasp. She slides her arms around his neck, presses her lips against his until her tongue flicks through to swirl inside the delicious tunnel of his mouth.

Her eyes open on the light from the streetlamp snaking up the wall. "Are you awake?"

"Inner clock's messed up. Must be two or three in the morning," he says.

"Some wine to help you sleep? A joint? I know, let's take a walk. No one's outdoors now."

"Don't want to mess up your system too."

But her feet have already hit the floor. Summer dressing is simple: pair of shorts, T-shirt, and sandals. In a few hours, she'll have to change for work. Worry about that later. Having him home is cause for a celebration that shouldn't be slept away.

"Wear your Mexican whatever those shoes are called." Now it's she who is energetic, more than that, revived, the flap down on the tent of her worries at least for a while. They made love twice, the second time slowly. She's still wrapped in the warmth of it.

They tiptoe down the stairs into the humid air. Infrequent traffic sounds interrupt the middle-of-the-night silence. Claiming the sky as their private property, she searches the navy-blue blanket for stars. They head to Riverside Park. It's wondrous to be with the person you love, she thinks.

On a bench they sit close together, a slight breeze rustling the tree leaves. Her eyes examine the dark bushes for evidence of life. A patrol car passes slowly, and the two cops inside stare at them. For a miserable moment, she fears the cops will stop and ask questions, but they drive on. "Assholes," she mutters.

"Cursing isn't going to change the racist fabric of closed minds. Waste of energy, Josie. I learned much from the Vietnamese in Cuba. They make a great distinction between the people and the government, which sometimes we forget to do. They also taught me that small attitudes are the last to change."

"Are you saying cops are the people?"

"Not particularly, just that white radicals don't always make distinctions. Symbolism is more important to you than it is to our people."

"Do you think the draft board was symbolic?"

"Yeah, I heard about that. It's only a slap at government property. It sure doesn't organize people to change their lives, right?"

His words mirror her feelings, but with Miles taking up space in her head, she says nothing.

"That's why the Panther breakfast, prison, and clothing programs are so important. They offer material aid while demonstrating how life should be, which pisses off the Man, who is afraid of revolutionary examples, see? Anyway, it's the people who make revolution, not a handful of radicals. The difference between Black and white radicals is that Black people are used to the long haul."

"Are you saying white radicals are just playing around?"

"I won't deny it."

These are distancing words. No, she mustn't read into them

more than that they've been away from each other too long; it's loosened the connection. She won't allow distance between them.

"I need to hear who you met, what you accomplished. Tell me." Her face upturned, a captive audience of one.

"So much happened. Where to begin . . . ? I don't know."

"The mission, you as emissary, what happened with that?"

"We opened a Panther office in Ghana, left two of our cadre there."

"Wow, impressive. Will you rotate people to Ghana?"

"We plan to send people into several of the countries."

"That must be so satisfying. Though, I did miss you. A lot." Her eyes on his remain steady, and he reads her, thank heaven. He pulls her close, kisses her forehead. She breathes in his familiar scent and thinks but isn't sure that the sky is beginning to brighten.

18

Melvin's atonal singing in the shower reminds her yet again that he's home. He's been back for over a week, and the joy of having him here hasn't receded. This morning they each spent a few hours in different corners of the apartment, Melvin writing his piece for the Panther newspaper, she an article for *Nation Magazine*. Then they took a walk in Riverside Park, where people were more interested in one another's dogs than an interracial couple. Now he's getting ready to attend another long Sunday night meeting in Harlem. Can she say, Phone me so I know the police haven't shot you?

Across the street from their apartment, two men sit inside a dark green sedan, which has been there for two days, maybe hoping Miles will visit. Melvin refuses to acknowledge its presence except to say, "Don't let them know you're bothered." But she is bothered. Why must they live under surveillance? Is this America or what?

Fingers tap at the door.

She looks through the peephole. "Celia!" Her sister meeting Melvin wasn't on today's agenda. She opens the door.

Celia steps inside hesitantly. "Hi. Was nearby." Her sister's eyes are puffy, red rimmed.

Melvin isn't going to stay in the shower much longer. She calls out, "We have company!"

"Roommate?" Celia asks.

"Melvin is his name." She's about to add that he's Black, but a wave of defiance or maybe plain weariness stops her.

Celia, who hasn't been here before, takes in the untidy room as if the space might offer answers to unspeakable questions.

Melvin walks out of the bathroom with a towel around his waist.

"This is my sister Celia."

"Oops." He grabs some clothes, hurries back in the bathroom. She glances at Celia, who stares at the closed bathroom door. In no time Melvin reappears in jeans and a T-shirt. And extends his hand to shake Celia's. Her sister reciprocates with no hesitation. Is this how change occurs?

"Truly a pleasure." He speaks in his oh-so-gallant voice. "I'd love to spend time with you, but I'm late for a meeting and regretfully have to run." He slips into his sandals. "See you later, baby." They kiss on the lips. Then he's out the door.

"Seems like a gentle guy," Celia says.

Gentle, a code word, but she won't take it on, won't say, You mean he's Black and not scary? "So what brings you here?" she asks.

Celia registers only the pewter sky and the clip-clip of her wedged shoes on the Manhattan pavement. Now what? Go home, eat, sleep, and wait for an appointment? It's what her sister advised. She didn't know Josie had a roommate, or was he a boyfriend?

It'll be dark soon. Lately, she prefers the night and its promise of sleep to the morning's reality: Out with Denise she drank too much and then went to bed with a guy she'd only just met. The putative father was drinking too.

She didn't find him attractive, just attentive, blond hair slick as a seal. He paid for the drinks, tipped the waiter, fed quarters into the music box. But it was his arms tight around her on the dance floor, even more than the whispered flattery, that won her response. He linked his fingers in hers and never left her side. A dizzying night and she still can't recall the route to the motel, only the clothes strewn on the floor, a few swigs from some bottle of what she can't remember either.

Passion is good, healthy, and shouldn't be penalized, Josie told her, adding that a woman should be able to go to her family doctor to have an abortion. It felt weird to ask her younger sister for help. But where else could she go? Terry? Her mother? Denise? Actually, she did think about telling Denise, but Denise can't keep a secret. The last thing she wants is for anyone at work—especially Artie—to learn about her predicament. That's what Josie called it, a predicament that would be resolved. She said that her friend Maisie knew doctors that provided abortions.

She didn't need a doctor to tell her she was pregnant. After three births there were too many recognizable signs to ignore. If Paul were around, he'd be 100 percent against getting rid of the pregnancy. But, shit, he's not. He doesn't get even a vote in her head, does he? If he hadn't taken off, the so-called predicament would've never occurred.

Even without Paul's input, she's been arguing with herself constantly: Have it; don't have it. What's another baby? She's an experienced mother, can soothe, comfort, allay fears, diaper, feed, cook, and talk on the phone all in the same hour. She can continue to work. She's done so three times; the fourth will be a cinch. She still remembers the silky feel of a baby nestling close to her body. And didn't her father always say each baby brings its own luck? But is she prepared to go through the ordeal again, diapers, formula, and sleepless nights? How would she pay for childcare? She couldn't. Paul was there to help out with each baby. And even when he wasn't, she had his emotional and financial support. Anyway, the people in her world know that Paul has left her. How would she explain a pregnancy to her sons? Not possible.

19

The car speeds across the George Washington Bridge. Celia sits in the back with her sister. Josie's friend Maisie is driving. The pace of it all has her reeling. Wasn't it only a day or so ago that she told Josie? Now she's being ferried to New Jersey to have an illegal procedure. She's never before done anything illegal. Either have the baby or become a criminal. Those are her choices. If family knew where she was headed, they'd be horrified. Is she horrified too? What does it matter? Probing her feelings isn't going to change the outcome of the journey.

Maisie found the doctor and made the appointment, and she's grateful. Then Maisie arrived at her place early today to pick her up and to reassure her that all would go well. A lonely heart needs friends, she thinks. Now, though, no one tries to make conversation, which is fine. She wants only to have the procedure over and done with, then a day of recovery and then back to work. With Quince at the Point and Miles not around, Sam is the only one she had to lie to. He believes she's having a small growth removed, and he's staying at Maria's.

They park in the driveway of a big house with a spacious, well-tended lawn on a quiet street with only a few other well-turned-out houses. A footpath leads to the front door, where Celia marks the moment as she always does when something irrevocable is about to happen. Three steps up and they're inside. It's not a waiting room. It's a living room, with a shiny piano, prints on the wall, a couch, and silky flowers in a vase. Suddenly, she wants to turn around, go home, try and solve the problem another way. She's a good problem solver, always has been. She . . .

Josie takes her hand, tugs her gently through a long hallway to another, smaller room.

The doctor looks old, maybe in his seventies. He says nothing to welcome her. He's in shirt-sleeves. He has square, spatula-like fingers. Where's his white jacket? What about sterility, bandages, heart monitors? What if there are side effects? What if her heart fails or she hemorrhages; how can that be dealt with? In the center of the room is a high flat table with stirrups, and beside it a small side table covered in a white cloth. Two nearby floor lamps are lit, but the room is dim, the window shade down.

He gives her a paper robe to leave open at the front, asks her to undress behind a two-panel screen.

The doctor helps her onto the table and then places her feet in the stirrups. She's cold.

"Move down as far as you can," the doctor instructs. Her legs are already so far apart each knee touches the edge of the table. It's uncomfortable. Her teeth are chattering, her body trembling; she's afraid of what's about to happen. But can't make herself ask the doctor for a shot, a blanket. She's a good girl who's been a bad girl and now must pay for it without complaint.

"Josie?" she whispers. "I want to be asleep for this."

Josie grips her hand.

"It won't be long, and without anesthesia you'll feel a hundred percent better afterward," the doctor advises.

Clearly, he wants her out of his home as soon as the abortion is done. Can she blame him? But what if she screams. What then?

"I'm nauseated," she whispers. "I might need to vomit."

"You'll be fine," the doctor intones, no doubt having said these words too many times to feel like they matter. But she won't be fine. Something colder than ice is inside spreading her vagina beyond what's bearable. Who would choose to go through this unless they had to? She moans, and it sounds like the feeble call of a sick bird.

Promising that she'll rest, she insists that Josie go home. That Sam will be having dinner at his friend's house, and, yes, she'll phone Josie if there are any untoward side effects. Glad to see her sister out the door, she pours herself a glass of wine and lies on the couch, her mind dizzy with too many thoughts. How can she be sure she's no longer pregnant? Not a good question. She knows what it takes to give birth, yet the abortion lasted no more than thirty minutes. There's some bleeding and cramping, but after three births it doesn't feel serious. At work, the women often share gory stories about how to get rid of an early pregnancy, though abortion isn't mentioned. Then again, abortion isn't cheap. Hers cost a few hundred dollars that she borrowed from the rent money. How to make that up is something she still needs to work out.

Closing her eyes, she thinks: It's done. She'll make herself forget the whole ordeal . . . except she can't; it's hers to remember. It wasn't a seedy room, a filthy house, or a waiting area filled with the tension of women. Rather, it was efficient, which can feel more terrifying: a thirty-minute illegitimate procedure with no one to smooth the way in or out of the event. And—

The phone rings.

"Hello."

"Hi, it's Maisie. Wanted to know how you're doing. Do you need anything? Food? Company? A book? I could drop over."

"How sweet. But no, I'm resting. I don't need anything."

"How's your body doing? I mean, are you in pain or—"

"Just very tired."

"That's usual."

"You know that because . . ."

"I've friends who have gone through abortions. No procedure is great, but what makes an abortion feel more awful is that it's secret and treated as something illicit."

"Yes. It did feel sneaky, even dirty, though the house was clean. A hospital would've made it feel more valid."

"You have my number?"

"I do. Maisie, thanks for everything."

Maisie's words rescued her, from what she's no longer sure.

Probably September

Remember City Island, Josie? Remember Fourth of July? How disorganized and hot it was on that pier? Multiply that by a zillion, and you still won't have a sense of any night here. Think about being always on guard for what may or may not come. Then imagine the nights filled with deafening, ear-piercing noise followed by throat wrenching, gut ripping screams—how else to know we're alive?—and you get a taste of it here, but just a baby spoonful. It's a circus, a freak show. Anything can happen and it does. Ignited by flares, we're silhouettes in a shooting gallery, and only God and Ho Chi Minh know how many eyes are peering from all the tangled growth. The grim reaper's our partner. He can't be outsmarted, no sir. Just hold on to faint hope his decision about you hasn't been made yet. However, enough booze and even death takes a vacation.

Everyone's stoned out of his mind, and thank God for that. Shucking off the sons of bitches ants in a hash haze saves sanity. The heat is unbearable with clothing on, but who wants to expose flesh to those mother-sucking mosquitoes? You want to know what we put up with? It's more than the VC, because Charlie's invisible during the day and hidden at night, and unless you're paranoid enough to take out some farmer working his rice field, it's the jungle itself. Man, how do these people exist here?

And it's frustrating trying to describe a day in the life, like painting a picture without paint. So why bother? I mean, what's in it for me if anyone gets the scene? Even *people's letters sometimes give me a headache. Johnny's salute—here's to you, kid—while he's at home drinking scotch and watching the Yankees does less than zip for me. And my friend Gretta is still writing to that guy, Richie, who made his car keys dance on the bar, but who is he? Her sweet, silky, sexy words, meant to be affectionate, provide a brief moment of porn. Thing is, I can't respond in kind, not yet, maybe never, and in truth I don't worry about it. And your letters, Josie, I grant you they're easier on the eye than the shit in <u>Stars and Stripes</u>. Still, the stuff you relate . . . I mean . . . women fighting macho men—how could that possibly matter to me here? And the millions of people you claim are hoofing it against the war, how does that affect the carnage? None of it adds up to one body saved. None of it cools the landscape, fumigates the ants, or blocks incoming. And I don't care anymore if it's Johnson, Nixon, or King Tut as president, because no one knows how to end the siege even if they wanted to, which they don't. Otherwise they'd sign any damn peace treaty tonight instead of pussyfooting around. Can you believe it? Blood and guts and bodies all over the fucking place and they argue words? Send them over here so we can shoot the lot of them.*

About now you're thinking that I'm three sheets to the wind and you're half-right. I've smoked some weed, downed a few beers, softened my arteries with swigs of rotgut. Then again, dulling the senses is what it's about. I know I haven't written you for a while, busy saving up the bits and pieces, but try as I might, I can't come close to your six/seven pages worth of words, no way. But also, and really, other than assuring you I'm alive (in a way), it's the same shit this month as last month and the month before. It's not that I have the need to be poetic or some such crap. But I do have enough pride not to want to be seen as the dumb soldier boy who can't find anything of value to say. Except I can't, not often, because though I'm not dumb, I am soldiering and what that means here you don't really need to know, no matter how many times you claim you do.

You take care, Josie. I can't worry about your safety too.

Love,
Richie

-20-

With his arm heavy across her chest, his lips rest on her neck.

"Can I move?" Josie asks.

"Mmm. Too comfortable." He rolls over on his back.

"Are you needed at the breakfast program this morning?"

"Yeah. I have a table of little goofy jumping jacks. Five or six of them belong to the Panther sisters."

"What about the Panther brothers?"

"Okay, smartass, but it takes too long to lay out an entire biography."

"Would you want to have children?" How come she doesn't know this?

"Is this a lead-in question?"

She can sense his tension. "Of course not. God forbid. I was just curious if you liked kids."

"I think about it."

"What does that mean?"

"Well . . . on the one hand, the more of us there are, the safer we'll be."

"On the other hand?"

"Is this like a need to know? I mean, right now?"

"Everything I ask I need to know." He doesn't want her to pursue this. A list of reasons she doesn't want to read run in a headline around her brain.

"Yes . . . that's so true, Josie."

"Don't sound so exasperated."

"I'm aiming for the shower. Though I want to nuzzle you all over again, I have no time to provide answers to your pithy questions." He nips her ear and then slides his legs off the side of the bed.

He likes kids; she knows he does. Having one with a white woman, though, that may not be on his agenda. She understands. They live in a country that makes normal happenings feel abnormal. Anyway, having children isn't on her agenda.

"Come back. I have a little while before I have to get dressed for work." She doesn't want the morning to end, doesn't want to think about the day ahead or Lowell's message, which she hasn't shared with Melvin. He already thinks white radicals are too full of themselves. The message included instructions on how to make sure that she wouldn't be followed. Was that necessary, she wonders, or are the layers of secrecy a way to make activists feel important?

"Josie, if I climb back . . . never mind." His long, lean torso disappears into the bathroom.

Daylight has crept into every corner of the shadeless room. She slips out of bed, wraps the sheet around her, and stands at the open window. A cool breeze hints at autumn, her favorite season, though it's when things begin to die.

Exiting the last subway car, she takes in as many faces as she can of those who also get off. Then enters a nearby pharmacy, walks through the aisles, and watches to see if anyone from the train has followed her in. No one she recognizes, which is what she expected.

In the hospital lobby, she buys the newspaper and a container of coffee, then heads to the second-floor offices. Everything must be as usual. In a few hours, a fugitive will arrive here, where nurses bustle in and out of rooms and doctors route the sick to heaven.

At twelve thirty, her lunchtime, she takes the elevator up to the sixth floor cafeteria, which is as large as a basketball court and open to the public. Trays are piled high near the counters; women in white hairnets and pink dresses ladle out the hot foods.

She slides a tray along the rails, picks up a sandwich and a drink, then finds a vacant table for two. The cafeteria is crowded and the buzz of voices loud, but fortunately, none of her coworkers are nearby.

Miles slips into a chair across from her and places a tray with a garden salad and some napkins on the table. He's dressed in slacks, sport jacket, and tie, his crew-cut hair dyed light brown. Only his dark eyes are recognizable behind the wire-framed glasses. "Hi," he says, but couldn't sound more indifferent.

Is he supposed to be a stranger, a friend, a colleague, or what? No one has said. "It's nice to see you," she replies carefully.

He nods.

Though she can't tell him about Celia's abortion or that Celia plans to attend an upcoming abortion rights meeting, she can keep a promise. Leaning across the table to reach for one of his napkins, she whispers, "Celia needs to meet with you. She'll do whatever you ask to make it happen."

"Not a good time." His quick whispered response a crystal-clear message.

"Celia doesn't care what you do about the draft," she persists.

"The draft is the least of my problems." His eyes remain on the food.

"Give me a note for her?"

"Can't." An icy-toned warning not to pursue this.

There's much she'd love to share with him: about the Panther 21, about the call for reparations and more. But he's busy shoveling every last bit of salad into his mouth, a camel preparing for a desert crossing.

"I bumped into my cousin Grace. She's living with her lover, a woman."

"A lesbian?"

"Is that all you can say? What's the matter with you?"

"Sorry," he mumbles. But is he? She's confused. What's real here, she needs to know. It's Miles, sweet, daring Miles. Is he keeping a distance from her the way that doctors learn not to get deeply involved with patients in order to survive their deaths? Is that what Miles is doing? Surviving love, his mother's and hers?

"How's the job going?" he suddenly asks as if they've been discussing this all along. "Did you get that raise? I never received mine, so I'm skimping now. Cash has become a problem."

Beneath the casual words, there's urgency. Money is the reason for the meeting. She can't refuse him, though there's a bottom to her cash. She removes bills from her purse and places them under a napkin, which disappears quickly.

"Need to go, can't be late for work. Good seeing you."

She watches him disappear through the exit door. The meeting leaves her poorer, bewildered, even angry. The tiptoe carefulness, the evasiveness, what does any of it mean? And what about her sister? Will it relieve Celia to know that she met with Miles or upset her that he refuses to see her?

-21-

"Bye, sweet girl."

"Bye." Josie replaces the receiver. Melvin's more excited than she's heard him sound in weeks. Several Panthers, including two of the women, are free on bail raised by his defense fund. This after being imprisoned on made-up conspiracy charges of planning to bomb New York City buildings. Melvin's on his way to escort the Panthers to a party in their honor at the attorney's town house.

At least now maybe he can stop the frantic fund-raising. No doubt another project awaits him. How dangerous will that one be? A question she won't ask, because he cautions that the less she knows about certain projects, the better. About everything else, though, he talks a mile, including anecdotes.

Unfortunately, the celebration interferes with her plan to spend the evening alone with him. She wants to share yesterday's meeting with Miles, get his feedback on what might be going on. Miles has been on her mind nonstop. But she suddenly needs to shake herself into a party mood, whatever that might be.

Glancing out the window, she wonders if any of the people on the street think her thoughts, fear her fears, or experiences sudden premonitions of danger like the one that now grabs her by the throat. It's as if someone is whispering something to her that she can't quite hear.

The three-floor Greenwich Village town house is tucked into a private mews. It has a large backyard with a children's playground that's more equipped than most city parks.

Entering the long foyer, she's met by a cacophony of voices and a young woman carrying a tray of wineglasses. She helps herself to a glass and then saunters through several enormous rooms, all with cathedral ceilings and long linen-covered, food-filled tables. People from everywhere crowd the spaces, including a few TV cameramen. The sumptuous surroundings bring to mind Radio City Music Hall, where her third-grade class went on a field trip. The high ceilings, the chandeliers, standing amid the gilt trimming in the majestic auditorium with its velvet seats, it dazzled her. She felt like a person in someone's painting.

"Sweet pea, I've been searching for you." Ben kisses her cheek. "You rule in that dress, Josie." It's Nina's beige silk T-strap mini; Nina tires easily of clothes.

"Lots of people here," she says.

"Is this not a red-white-and-blue day?"

"I wouldn't say it quite that way."

"The people have spoken with their wallets, my pretty friend. They won't stand for the chicanery of the justice system. That's progress, and it makes me fly."

He's wearing the scent of cannabis like aftershave. But she smiles, because he means every word, and his light heart is contagious.

"Let's you and me celebrate," he says. "We'll board the Manhattan ferry, stare at the Statue of Liberty, and smoke pot."

"An invitation to consider. Let me get back to you."

"I've heard that before. By the by, what's going on with Nina and Lowell?" he asks.

"How do you mean?"

"Why isn't she here with him? He's roaming the rooms like a man without a country."

"She'll probably arrive with her women's group. Anything wrong with that?"

"Don't twit my basket, Josie. It's Lowell that's patrolling the hallways; maybe you should enlighten him."

"What'll you do now that the defense committee needs less time?" she asks.

"I'll retire next door to Nixon so I can continue to harass him. Actually, a bunch of us are traveling up the East Coast with a group of Native Americans to introduce their movement on the campuses. Want to come?"

"No, I'm helping to set up organizing committees in white working-class areas of the city. We'll bring in people to talk about the war, racism, childcare, et cetera. A few of my friends plan to move into the neighborhoods, organize from a collective base."

"Will you move too?"

"No. I'll work with them from the outside."

"It's what you've wanted to happen for a while, isn't it?"

His words surprise her. She didn't think he ever took her wishes seriously.

"Was it so apparent?"

"At every meeting a remark about what should be happening that isn't." He grabs her hand, tugs her toward the backyard. But she resists, wanting to be inside when Melvin arrives.

"Waiting for the supreme entrance, are you? I'm about to blow some smoke, so if you change your mind . . ." He kisses her again, then ambles off, checking his pockets for ingredients.

The room has gotten noisier, the atmosphere pervaded with a sense of energy and expectation. Add to that the pungent aroma that could be mistaken for incense only by someone new to this world. Wouldn't Miles love to be here? But he can no longer be seen among them. She admires his sacrifice, she truly does, and wonders if she'd have his courage. And yet, she can't find it in herself to uncritically support his action, though she's no pacifist. Thinking about him, it occurs to her that maybe it wasn't aloofness or evasiveness but fear that ruled their meeting yesterday. Maybe he'd just received some horrific information. Didn't his tense body telegraph fear? Why did she miss that? She wanted them to be the way they'd always been when together and couldn't see past her own expectations. Of course he needs money. No doubt he must flee the country. She has to get another message to him.

To her surprise, Nina and Maisie enter the room with Celia, who's wearing a long dress of many colors that can't be hers.

Weaving through the crowd to reach her sister, she's saddened not to have a note from Miles. She links her arm with Celia's and pulls her aside.

"I didn't expect to see you here. I'm thrilled. Did Maisie persuade you? I mean—"

"Actually, she did, said free food and drink, so why stay in an empty apartment? It's true, about the empty place, especially now with Sam working after school and then studying at Maria's."

"Guess what? I bumped into our cousin Grace. She's as beautiful as a star and doing well. She asked me not to reveal that I met her to the extended family."

"Are you sure it was her?"

"Of course. What a silly question."

But Celia's face has paled. "Why is she staying hidden?"

"She's a lesbian, Celia. She has a lover, a woman."

"What?"

"Please don't say anything to make me sorry I told you. She has a right to live the way she wants."

"Everything is so simple to you." Celia's tone is sharp.

"Why should Grace have to lie? She is who she is, and so what?"

"How could you keep Grace a secret from her family? It's cruel. Do you realize what her absence does to them? They worry about her nonstop. They imagine her living in a drug den or homeless and begging for pennies. Grace owes her family some peace."

"Why are you so pissed?"

"Because of Miles, I share their trauma. Is he hungry, eating garbage, sleeping in subway cars? Can anyone tell me? Can you? You have no idea of the wretched, all-consuming pain."

Before she has a chance to respond, voices shout: "Power to the people!" "Live like them!" "Dare to struggle!" Fists shoot up, including hers; feet pound the floor with enough gusto to shake the chandeliers. There's applause as well. Melvin, in black chinos, white Nehru shirt, and a necklace of amber beads, leads in the Panthers. His eyes glow with triumph.

They decide to walk home from the party. Though fall has settled on its colors, it's a warm night with a slight breeze; wispy clouds travel the dark sky. Melvin jabbers away. He's feeling satisfied, expansive, energized.

Times Square is neon lit, marquees aglitter with the bright ferocity of a never-ending carnival. Huge billboards sell their wares. Tourists have their pick of myriad ethnic foods in glass-fronted restaurants. Winos walk the street; panhandlers sit on curbs holding out hats for money. Music spills from hidden clubs. Times Square is an event that insists on itself no matter the day or time.

When they reach Central Park West, where it's quiet, and Melvin has wound down some from his high, she tells him about her meeting with Miles. "And I don't know what to do for him. I want to help, though."

He says nothing.

"Have you heard about any trouble?"

"I don't know anything."

She detects annoyance. "Have you been in contact with him since . . . ?" Even here on empty cobbled streets with only the trees to hear, she's afraid to be explicit.

"I know how much he means to you, Josie, but he and I are part of separate struggles."

The words cut like a knife. "But you share goals," she insists.

"It's not advantageous for our people to interact with white fugitives. We can't afford more arrests or trials. Too much still to be done, and we need every Black warrior to do it. Even if I had the opportunity to meet with Miles, I wouldn't take it."

"But he's not another white guy, Melvin. He's your friend, your comrade, someone you hung with. He must've helped you with the stuff that never arrived in the coffeehouse, right? And now that he's in trouble, he's just another white fugitive? I don't get it."

"You're right. Miles is a special guy, a great guy, but the struggle for Black liberation is at a critical juncture, and I know you know that. There'll come a time when some of us will have to disappear as well, and we'll need the help of those who've already successfully done so. But for now the requirements in the Black community are above ground and foremost. Aiding white fugitives is not on the agenda at present."

"I understand, but doesn't that narrow the struggle? We need to widen it."

"Josie, girl, what do you mean when you say 'we'? Because not one of the Panther 21 is white. Not one of the seventeen Panthers killed so far is white. Not one of the apartments in the Harlem rent strike houses a white family. No white person frequents the neighborhood supermarket or the barbershop or even the liquor store, yet white people own them. Baby girl, listen, we're past the civil rights aspects of the struggle. Black people need to be more than beautiful. We need to feel the strength of our numbers and move in tandem. That's where we are today. Tomorrow, next year, five years from now, we'll be elsewhere, but today we have to deal with today."

Some things are too fragile to touch, too delicate to handle at all.

"Celia," Artie calls from the doorway of his glass cage, "phone."

She hurries to his office refusing to think about who would be calling her at work. "Hello."

"Mom?" It's Quince's earnest voice. "We saw Pop . . . me and Sam . . . He's quite ill . . . St. Vincent's Hospital . . . One of the nuns wrote to me at the Point . . . Didn't know whether to tell you, because, Mom . . . he doesn't want you to visit him."

Artie is trying not to pay attention. "Okay, Quince honey, thanks for letting me know. We'll talk later. I'm at work now." She hangs up and can feel Artie watching her as she returns to her station to finish out the last two hours.

In the early-evening darkness, she makes her way down Seventh Avenue South to Twelfth Street, Quince's words alive in her head. Propelled by an invisible hand, she refuses to focus on the destination.

One of the women in her new group would've gone with her if she'd asked, but their pasts are so different from hers: none of them have children; none were married as young as she was. How could they understand? She grew up with Paul.

The hospital is housed in a large, old building, the plate-glass front grimy and the lobby a bit seedy. She's early. Visiting hours won't start for another fifteen minutes.

The stuffy waiting area reminds her of a long-ago day. Paul

swept up in the arrest of several band members in a drug bust, though at the time he hadn't been using. It was winter, Miles just a year old. Bundling him into a snowsuit, she carried him to the precinct, where she waited for Paul's release for hours in a dim windowless room while Miles cried or fussed. She was furious at Paul for putting her through that misery. When, finally, he emerged, she thrust Miles at him and was about to flee. He grabbed her and, with Miles between them, wrapped his arms around her, whispered, "Hey, my lady, thanks. I love you to the moon," his voice low, sexy, his breath close, his eyes steady on her. Why was it always enough?

Curtains are drawn around each of the three cubicles in the room. He's in the bed near the window. He's covered with a sheet, his head propped high on pillows, his eyes closed. An oxygen tank stands guard nearby. An IV drips slowly into his arm. His thin face is barely recognizable, the bones too prominent beneath paper skin. A blue shadow stretches around his chin. She doesn't wake him but stands at the window, the silence strangely reverent.

Quince didn't mention Paul's changed appearance. Maybe a father's a father no matter how he looks. What about a husband? When she turns around, his eyes are open, staring at her. But gone is the old electricity, as if his story has already been told.

She smiles.

"Hey, lady."

"I heard you didn't want me to visit, so I came."

"Didn't want you to see me," his voice weak, breathy.

"I've seen you worse," she lies.

"Maybe . . . in a nightmare, I suppose."

"Are you in pain?"

He shakes his head. "Come closer."

She pulls a chair to the bed. "You shouldn't have walked out on us." The words emerge without a plan.

"Yeah, it was bad, the needle . . . the only companion I could suffer."

"I figured that."

"Miles . . . haven't seen him. Saw Quince, Sam." His slim fingers weakly tap the sheet, and she wonders if there's still music in his head or if that, too, is gone.

"Miles has disappeared. He's running from the draft."

He nods, words a waste of breath.

She could chat about their sons, or she could reveal how each day after he left was filled with scary questions whose answers eluded her. Or she could tell him about her new women friends and how they've opened up other ways to think about ancient worries. Or she could admit she isn't as unhappy as she thought she'd always be. That she understands at last how love has its limits, that two halves do not make one whole couple, and how, anyway, he was never hers to lose. But his mind is elsewhere, the stuff of life no longer of interest. Perhaps he's finally carefree. How ironic.

He turns toward the window. "I'm dying, lady."

She slides her hand over his cool fingers and follows his gaze. A few scudding clouds, a building fragment, pigeons perched on an eave, their iridescent colors muted. How mysterious . . . the stories left to share all shelved like forever unopened boxes after a move.

"When it's over, I'll feel nothing. Can't be scared of nothing," he offers in a slow, whispery tone.

The sky is darkening, and so is the room, but there's no need to turn on a light. If he were less, fragile she'd rest her head on his chest and wonder why later. For now, she keeps hold of his hand.

"You'll be all right," he whispers, and it sounds like a promise.

November

*Josie, hi. It's my birthday. I know you know that. Tur-
key dinner from a can of rations plus all the goodies the
guys got from home dropped on my bed. Here's the thing:
I wasn't in a sweets mood. Here's another thing, about
which I do care. My brother-in-arms, Al, my buddy forever, no longer fears death. That's good. But that's about
the only good thing I can come up with, except it doesn't
really help. He got hurt bad, and well . . . he didn't make
it. Being with Al here on his second tour (which I never
understood before, and now I do and will explain later
if I remember), he was tired of being afraid, and I bet
he didn't fight to keep his eyes open, because peace here
means something very different than peace there where
you are struggling to get peace here. Ha-ha. Peace here
means not just ending fear but also stopping the thick,
spooky jungle silence that isn't at all silent. Peace here
means avoiding the dampness that makes you shake with
cold sweat and the constant itching and so forth and so
on. Peace here means gladly leaving earth for heaven and
has nothing to do with religion. I miss Al a lot, sure, but
I kind of envy him too. Here the concept of future slowly
recedes, and then one day it simply doesn't matter the way
it once did. I hope you don't understand what I'm trying
to say, because that would mean you were feeling like I
am. Or I don't like thinking about you in my shoes, as
the saying goes.*

 *The night I heard my buddy didn't make it or I be-
lieve didn't want to make it I got so high I couldn't find*

my socks, which is important. *Yesterday's sweaty socks cause mucho painful foot problems. It was a strange high, though. I mean, I've been high before, clearly. Only this time, with my buddy gone, or because of that, I wasn't able to forget his absence. I wanted to. I tried. I drank. I smoked weed/hash. I drank some more. Passed out, of course, which didn't stop me having to get up again knowing what I knew.*

The guys here say peace ain't gonna happen soon. Most of their predictions are bracketed with fuck or fucking, so I won't go into too much of the content. Except . . . there is growing, and I mean growing, resentment toward the brass. We get orders galore, one set more ridiculous than another. An example: check out the nearest village for VC. (That's slang for search and destroy.) What village? we look at each other and ask. They don't know. The LT doesn't know. The brass just wants to keep us busy so we don't have time to ponder the utter waste of our time. Like I said before but just remembered, I didn't understand why anyone in his right mind would want to come back here for a second tour. And no one in his right mind does come back, because by the end of your stint here, no one is in his right mind. Hope that wasn't too confusing. But I am of sound mind. Maybe. Nevertheless, listen carefully to what I have to say. I can't go home, not yet, and don't know when I can and can't explain it except that I can't leave here while it's still going on, so I'm staying. Okay, even if you're right and I've lost it, so what?

So yeah, it's my birthday and I was trying to remember if I ever had a birthday party at home. Except, Josie, I can't see home. Remember when I told you I couldn't hear Pa's voice in my head anymore? Well, here's another deficit. I can't picture home or even imagine having a slice of pizza and a beer as meaning anything like what it used to mean, which was simple pleasure. Because, sister, after time spent here . . . Well, it's like this: if you stare at the sun too long, all you can see for a while is a glare and nothing else. When I try to see, really see, Ma's don't-touch living room, it's a blur. When I try to visualize the block or the stores or the high school, it's a struggle. Thing is, I haven't been away a lifetime, but that's just it, Josie, that's exactly it. Over here a lifetime is spent in a day, and a day-after-day lifetime, well, it sure is wearing. There's no good way to explain any of this to anyone on this earth, let alone at home, especially if that person hasn't been where I'm standing.

Maybe because it's my day of birth, I ask myself: Who are these people in our family? I mean, I love them. How could I not? I mean, I'm supposed to. But I can no longer feel a part of family, because I can't remember what that actually felt like. It's true we take all of that for granted. But don't. On some nights, particularly when I'm out on patrol, I spend a lot of silent time trying to identify with each one of you. I know we all share the same shape of nose, but that's not enough. In a way the family have become strangers. You too, except your letters keep you up front, less distant, helped even more by your overly descriptive narratives (too much) of your activities. I see my devilish sister running from corner to corner trying to change everything between. I didn't say that, you did, in one of your recent letters.

You haven't mentioned Ma in your letters. Is she okay living at Johnny's? He's such a control freak, but maybe at her age she likes having everything taken care of. Except you know Ma. She has her own means of control, way different from Johnny's. I know, asking about them after telling you they are strangers must sound loony. But that's how I get through writing a letter, saying it as it comes out of my head, kind of free-associating, but very unclear about why one thought follows another. You did mention some mysterious shit about Miles being gone. Please be more specific, because mystery is the last thing I need to ponder. Oh, right, I started this letter because it's my birthday. If this is my most confusing letter, so be it.

So take care of you, don't worry about me, and yeah, I do like getting your letters. My fifty girlfriends have sort of given up on me. Ha-ha. But the few who were managing to stay in touch I fear must have gotten somewhat pissed at my attitude, and truthfully, I don't even know what that is.

Tell the gang hello and whatever else you feel like. Josie, don't get hurt.

Love you sister,
Richie

-23-

The Village is bewildering: curlicue streets, avenues without proper names. Searching for Grace's building on Carmine, she weaves around men clustered near smoldering trash cans, trying to stay warm and drinking from bottles hidden in paper bags.

Since the release of the Panthers a few days ago, she hasn't mentioned Miles again. The discussion she and Melvin had on the way home from the party remains painful to consider; she can neither erase it nor counter it. All she can do is abide. Somewhere she read that all movements for change demand uncomfortable individual adjustments of one kind or another.

Last night in bed, talking quietly about the day's events, Melvin told her the party promoted him to a higher level, which makes him happy. She said she was so proud of him. Didn't say that having a title makes him more of an FBI target. Black men have been hunted down for eons; now it's the fighters for Black liberation that have the feds' ardent attention. About to switch off the lamp, Melvin suddenly seized her in a tight embrace, held her for a minute without saying a word. It scared her.

Grace lives on the top floor. Climbing the dark staircase, Josie can't avoid the smells: pine detergent and urine. Grace agreed to let her use the apartment while she and Carla were at work. Prepared to lie about today's meeting, she didn't have to. Grace didn't ask. Perhaps her cousin assumed it was a secret or a tryst or simply wasn't interested. On the fifth floor, in a hidden cubby below the roof, she finds the key that Grace left for her.

Entering the large studio reminds her of the moment in *The Secret Garden* when the movie turns Technicolor. Furnished with blue- and yellow-shaded floor lamps, the room features a yellow couch, matching chairs, and a blue shag rug. Plants are everywhere, so, too, scented candles. A small niche of a kitchen with shiny appliances resides beneath a loft bed.

Lowering the wooden blinds, she snaps them shut. A rhythmic knock that she and Lowell agreed on sends her to the door.

"Whoa? Didn't expect such elegance in this building. Whose place is it?" Lowell slips out of his bomber jacket.

"My cousin and her lover's."

"What does he do?"

"He's a she."

"Oh."

"My cousin isn't the reason for our meeting. Miles is."

"What about him?" His tone noncommittal.

Is she wrong? Has Lowell lost touch with him? "I'm worried about Miles. I saw him recently."

"He met you?"

"Why so surprised?"

"You're family. He took a stupid chance."

"I'm a comrade just like you are."

"Yeah, yeah, sure, but he's in no position to take any risk."

His suddenly serious tone frightens her. "Tell me what you know. Please."

Lowell says nothing, drops into one of the chairs, his Mexican belt buckle shiny in the lamplight.

"He needs money. I gave him what I had. We were in a cafeteria. We couldn't really talk. I want to help him. Please, tell me what you know."

He stares at her, his angular face tense.

There's noise in the hallway. A door slams. Soon a radio or TV is turned on loud. A man's angry voice saying what, they can't make out.

"We shouldn't stay here long," Lowell advises.

"I agree. So. Please, tell me . . ."

He stands and steps close, then whispers, "An informer in his collective."

A cold fist of fear lodges in her stomach. "Why would an informer permit the bombing to take place?" Her voice as low as his.

"The informer joined the collective after the first action was completed. He was working with them on preparing the next one. When he procured explosives too quickly, the collective became suspicious. No one showed for the second action. The collective split up. No one returned to the apartment. Miles could be anywhere."

"Jesus and hell," she says in a rush. "He needs to get out of the country."

"I can't reach him. He contacts me. He probably needs a place to stay, maybe here. No, forget that; it's still family."

"Lowell, if you hear from him, let him know I'll raise money." She doesn't say Celia will need to be told the truth and put in touch with an attorney. The FBI will surely visit her.

"So, listen . . . You can do something for me." He slips on his jacket. "Nina wants to experience the single life. She wants me to move out of the apartment. We have a good thing together.

Why ruin it? Talk to her, raise some pertinent questions." His voice trails off self-consciously because asking for help isn't his thing.

"Nina must've thought through her decision. She isn't impulsive. It could turn out okay. A little fresh air in a relationship can't hurt." Actually, she's surprised and disappointed that Nina didn't share her plans.

"Look, I'm all for women's lib. It's a great struggle. I see how important it is, but Nina's going too far, becoming a fanatic, a man-hater or something. Next thing you know she'll be tossing out her jewelry and smoking cigars."

"Well, maybe she will and maybe she won't; either way, it's her choice, her life, her battle. You don't have to agree with it, but if I were you, I'd pretend."

-24-

Josie walks down the worn steps of the El train. Though the air is cold, it's not windy, which comforts her slightly, the way a light blanket helps with coziness. Celia didn't want to meet today; it's Saturday, chore day, but she persisted, offering to come up to the Bronx. She doesn't want to delay enlightening her sister even one day.

Last night, she longed to share with Melvin what she'd learned about the informer in Miles's collective. But she didn't share it. He'd made it clear that he didn't want to know stuff about Miles. She suffered her resentment in silence. Anyway, it's wrong to get hung up on personal well-being now when so many are grappling with leaving their comfort zones to perform the greater good. As one woman recently wrote, it isn't the time to read about romance.

She's on Tremont Avenue, one of the many Bronx streets she frequented on her way to school or the pizza place or just to hang around trading words with whoever else was hanging out. She'd stop in at the grocery, candy, or five-and-dime store, the latter no longer there. In its place a six-story gray brick building that already appears as tired as its shuttered windows. Every inch of the area was once etched in her brain. It was her neighborhood; she owned it. Though she would often think: Is this my whole world? It's so small.

Now the stores seem narrower, closer together, and less welcoming. The faces inside are of no one she recognizes. Is it that she hasn't been here in a while, or is this already her past? Isn't she too young to be visiting her past?

The Whitestone Bridge, though, remains, as it always has, visible to the eye from almost anywhere. No doubt beneath its height teens in parked cars still make out, the car being the best or maybe the only hope for privacy. When she was thirteen and in a car kissing a boy of sixteen, she turned her face and saw Richie in the next car with a girl she couldn't identify, because he was on top of her. It upset her. But she could never decide if it was that her brother might have seen her or because of what she had viewed.

Grace, who knows this neighborhood as well as she does, has no desire to visit it again. Her cousin is considering contacting her mother, though concerned that a negative response to the word "lesbian" would upend her.

The strangeness of families, she thinks heading to meet Celia, a nest of vipers urging members to step into the same minefield again and again and a garden of angels ready to welcome any wayward child.

℘   ℘   ℘

The coffee shop is busy and noisy. Waiter's call out food orders as dirty dishes clatter perilously into aluminum bins. Glad to find a small empty booth, she orders coffee and waits impatiently for her sister to arrive.

The waiter, with a pitcher of water in one hand and a coffeepot in the other, fills her glass, then her cup. She feels self-conscious taking up a booth by herself while people wait for a place to sit and orders an English muffin and coffee for Celia, who soon hurries in, her pained expression alarming.

"What is it?"

"Richie," comes Celia's rough whisper.

Terror floods her body, her normal voice lost somewhere.

"Wounded," Celia says. "Shrapnel along his entire right side . . . affected the nerves. Some paralysis and lots of tremors, which they don't believe will disappear . . . Said that his condition isn't yet stable. The letter was sent to Ma. Terry phoned me crying. I ran over there to stay with Ma until Johnny came home." Celia's tone low, weary, her eyes narrowed in misery.

Richie, her Richie, the brother she loves most . . . who made her laugh, shared his candy, took her to the movies, who used to stand her on a chair to practice his boxing with her, though he never hit her, who taught her to dance, who . . . Her Richie, her very own brother. Could she hate the war more than she already does? And she pleads to the goddess of good people that he get better.

To ask Celia to share more details of the letter would be like demanding a drowning woman recite her social security number. Details don't matter; she needs to go to him. She'll leave at once for D.C. Isn't that where they send wounded soldiers? "Where exactly is he?"

"A hospital in Germany. When he's well enough to travel, he'll return stateside to be mustered out at some base. They're doing everything for him, I'm sure." Celia's trying to be reassuring, but the sorrowful tone belies the words. "I should go. Sam will be wondering where I am. Oh, wait, you needed to see me. Why?"

With Richie heavy on their hearts, it feels awful to have to share news about Miles, but what choice does she have?

"It's about Miles," she says gently. "Miles, well, he . . ." And the tale unfolds from the bombing of the draft board up to and including what Lowell told her, a story made simple with a beginning and middle but no end. "If FBI agents come to your house or place of work, you absolutely cannot talk to them. You may tell them the name of your attorney, which I'm about to give you."

Celia stares past her, a napkin balled tight in her hand.

The bus speeds through the dark night. It isn't far to her place. Celia could've walked from the coffee shop, but there was the bus and she got on. Her thoughts too jumbled to sort. She envisions seven-year-old Miles tugging her outside to check if the unmoving cat near the garbage can is alive. "If it's breathing," Miles said most determinately, "we must take him inside and heal him." More likely dead, Celia thought, and prepared him for the inevitable. Still, he insisted she inspect the mangy cat's pulse. Touching the neck, she affirmed the cat was gone. Though she expected him to ask, Gone where? he just stood there, and she remembers feeling guilty, as if somehow she'd let him down.

She wants him with her not in a memory but in person. His hating the war, yes, she understands that, but to such an extreme, so violent? What about consequences? Did they enter his mind? He's a fugitive. He could be shot on any street or sent to jail for the rest of his life. Doesn't he care about his future? How dare he be so careless with her? Except she isn't a factor, which cuts deep; still, his wildness, his passion, the intensity of his devotion, they stagger her. Where do they come from? She wills herself to face the fact: her firstborn is an enemy of the state. But he's also her son, and what's done is done, and she must hide her sorrow behind a mask of the ordinary.

Across the aisle a man old enough to be her father is riffling through photos, smiling now and then. He's not thinking about the FBI, but she must. The attorney's name is written on a card in her purse. Instructions must be followed. Josie forbade her to share anything with anyone and she won't, except for his brothers, because they, too, need to protect Miles. It's what families do.

The empty apartment feels suddenly unfamiliar. She closes her eyes for a moment to allow it to return to its usual self. But nothing is usual with Richie in the hospital, perhaps in pain. So many more wounded soldiers daily, so many more wives and parents saying, At least he's alive. It's how she feels too. But is that how Richie sees it? So much that he loves lost to him: dancing, running, even driving. And will he ever be able to have sex with a lover? What does being alive mean to someone who has seen too much dying for any one life?

Richie never had it in him to kill. She's always believed this. At age nine he owned a water pistol that he used against his make-believe enemies. One day at recess, he shot the water pistol in a boy's face, which blurred the boy's glasses. Richie said the boy went blind and demonstrated how the boy groped desperately for something to wipe the lenses. The next day Richie tossed the pistol, claimed that it no longer worked.

Melvin will be home, but when she isn't sure. She could phone Maisie or Ben to keep her company. Or she could have a drink or light up a joint or both, except it would feel like a cop-out. In one of his letters, Richie wrote that Johnny drinking scotch and watching a Yankee game did nothing for him. She wants to do something for him, but what? Maisie told her that Orthodox Jewish people tear their clothing to express grief for the deceased. Yet how to express her sorrow feels beyond her.

She's awake when Melvin gets home and tearfully tells him about Richie. Though it's two in the morning, he heats water for tea and garnishes it with a large dollop of scotch from a bottle they keep under the sink for emergencies. Then admonishes her not to get lost in worst scenarios, that some of the best medical treatments are discovered during war, and that, unlike here, the sick and wounded receive amazing care in the military. He says Richie won't die. How does he know? If Richie's made it to Germany, he's going to survive, he assures her.

Snatches of dawn light fracture the gunmetal sky as she sits down to write Richie a letter. It's filled with Melvin's assertions about military treatment, along with much advice from her about needing to believe in his ability to heal. Though she intends to write him every day, his trembling hand will no longer allow him to reply. In honor of Richie, she'll attend tomorrow night's antiwar demonstration in Manhattan, though what he'd think about that she isn't sure.

Police spotlights illuminate Sixth Avenue. It's dark and cold as Josie enters one of the crowded streets near the hotel where Nixon is scheduled to address a ballroom filled with millionaires. Thousands of people are crowding the area shouting slogans, blowing whistles, or banging drums. Someone throws a rock, smashing a bank window; others see this as permission, and soon rocks and cans are taking aim at any window in sight. The police are let loose. Protesters flee every which way. Culprit or not, escape is all.

Out of breath from running, she finds a doorway in which to stop a minute with two others. Their rest is cut short by police rushing in their direction. Before she can bolt, a hand collars her jacket. A club thwacks her shoulder, her ribs, the small of her back. Pain radiates up her neck like a flash fire. When she turns to see her assailant, the club catches her nose, and blood gushes. For a second, the young cop's hard button eyes glint with fear. She drops to her knees, presses her face against her thighs, arms crossed over her head. Seconds pass. No more blows. She needs to move before someone comes to arrest her. She crawls to another building and sits in the hallway as blood from her nose stains her jeans, shoes, socks. Her jaw is sore. After a minute or two, she hoists herself upright, squeezes the bridge of her nose to stem the bleed, and as fast as she can, makes her way toward home.

Still afraid, though no one is following her, she hurries. She's attended too many demonstrations to count but never before been beaten. Is this an omen for her, for the movement, for something more she can't quite get her head around? Violence doesn't recede; it escalates. When Nina was beaten at a demonstration, she was so outraged: How dare they touch her? How could they? Unlike Nina, she feels vulnerable, frightened.

As she reaches Central Park West, her breathing steadies some. The nosebleed has stopped. The streetlights glisten like a thousand sparklers. The cars pass as if in a silent movie. Is this what the aftermath of trauma is like? Is this what Richie felt? But her wounds will heal.

Only the whooshing in her ears is close, a sound that reminds her of the empty beach where her father took her on her tenth birthday. It was late autumn and a chilly twilight. She loved sitting on the sand listening to him describe how everything in his childhood smelled of the sea, sweet and salty, obliterating street fumes. Only then did she realize how much he missed the old country, nostalgia suddenly stamped on his face.

Pushing open the heavy front door of the building, she heads for the stairs. Hanging on to the railing, her legs two pieces of clay, she climbs each flight slowly. The hallways are devoid of the usual TV voices. It must be late. Her keys are on a string around her neck, but her finger presses the bell, willing Melvin to open the door. Her bloody self a badge of honor. How adolescent is that?

"Shit, Josie, baby, what happened?" But he's not waiting for answers. He's pulling her into the bathroom, running water, dipping towels. There's ice in a bowl brought in from the kitchen. She sits on the toilet seat letting him pat and dry and even opening her mouth for him to inspect her teeth. He tells her what to do and she obeys. "Hold the ice here." "Put the towel there." "Don't move." His breath tickling her face; his hands fiddling with her hair trying to pin it on top of her head. There are easier ways, but she says nothing, and he continues to do what needs to be done. She watches as he draws a bath. "Very hot," he tells her, "good for you." She watches as he peels off her clothes, which fall in a bloody heap. He's caring for her the way a doctor would, concerned, attentive, but no kisses or hugs.

His hand steady on her arm, he eases her into the water, then sits on the rim of the tub. No crying, not while he's ministering to her.

"Chipped bottom tooth, soft tissue damage in the nose, not broken. Check out how the jaw feels tomorrow. Anyway, it's going to be fine, Josie, you'll see, a blip as time passes." In his voice she hears years of reassuring injured friends.

In bed, she takes a deep breath, which surely hurts. Is that why he isn't trying to hold her?

Her eyes open on the morning light. She didn't hear the alarm. It's a little before eight. Her body aches as a beaten body does. The bed is empty. Melvin left earlier than usual. Why is that? she wonders. Then sees the envelope next to her pillow; its faint pencil marks read, "From Lowell." The sealed envelope is as light as air, but whatever is inside will be much heavier.

The motel facade looks as grim as the gray sky. As she searches for room number twenty-four among the look-alike doors, her heart's hammering reaches a dangerous level. Yesterday's beating has left her dogged by anxiety and with a shattered sense of immortality. Pulling herself together to come here was no picnic. Her back sends pain signals with each step, but she had to come. It's today or who knows when.

She taps lightly on motel door twenty-four.

Miles lets her in. His frizzy reddish hair and moustache startle her, and his eyes behind smoky-gray granny glasses are unreadable. He seems altered, older, sterner, his boyhood only a memory.

After a long hug during which they hold each other tightly, she doesn't trust herself to speak. She sits in a vinyl chair. He perches on the side of the bed. It's a small square room with a dresser, a TV, blinds snapped shut, and drapes that can be drawn to keep out the light. A black canvas gym bag sits on the floor, no doubt everything he owns inside it.

"Were you careful coming here?" he asks.

"Absolutely."

"Good."

"I need to tell you this first. Your father . . . he's in the hospital, very ill."

"Jesus Christ. How can I visit him? It would be a perfect trap." His tone pleading.

"I understand. No one wants you caught." She doesn't say he'll regret the decision. Not seeing her father before he died left her forever sorrowful.

"Did you visit him?" he asks.

"Not yet. Your brothers and your mother did."

"Do you have any more information about his condition?"

"I don't. Celia just said he's very weak."

"How's my mom?" he asks.

"Celia knows the whole deal about you. I connected her with an attorney."

"Such a burden," he murmurs more to himself.

"She can't touch, see, or hear you; that's her burden."

He says nothing.

"Richie was wounded and is in a German hospital." Her throat tightens.

"Shit. That's awful. At his farewell party, he couldn't wait for the night to end so his new life could begin." He shakes his head.

The family party she missed to attend her first DC demonstration, the one where she met Melvin. She now remembers telling herself again and again then that it was no big deal to miss a family gathering. Was she rationalizing or denying? What's the difference?

"What happened to your face?" He peers over his glasses.

In the mirror this morning, she saw what he sees now: a yellow-green stain below her puffy eye, swelling around her nose and upper lip. What he can't see is how each thwack of the club replays in her head. What no one speaks about, including her, is the rising fear of attending actions. "Yesterday at a Nixon demo, the cops charged. It's getting nastier out there every day."

"Yeah, I can imagine." It's clear he has no wish to be drawn into the streets.

"How are you, I mean, really?" she asks.

He looks at her for a long moment. "I'm as fine as I can be."

"That's no answer."

"Josie, it'll have to do. There's little I can tell you that you haven't probably already thought about. Hold on to the fact that I'm not sorry but don't want to be caught."

"You hold on to the fact that you are important to me and I'll do whatever I can to help you."

"I know that," he says quietly.

"I collected two hundred dollars from friends. Use the money to go to Canada."

He takes the money eagerly. "I will. After the next action, which is already planned."

"You can't mean that. It's too dangerous. They're looking for you, watching every draft board in the country."

"There are ways around all of it." He looks past her.

"It's too close to the last action . . . If you delay . . ."

"Another few thousand records destroyed, lives saved, what's more important than that?" His tone serious.

"How can you be certain they won't be waiting for you? You've been identified. You're known."

"It's been worked out. Trust me."

She's not one to be superstitious, but Christ, another action is more than daring; it's reckless. "What good is it to anyone if you're in prison?"

"The only way now to stop the war is to cause damage to the state."

"Damaging government property isn't the same as damaging the state," she says, parroting Melvin.

"If they're taken down one after another, the war will be denied cannon fodder."

"You're not indispensable. It can happen without you."

"Actually, it can't. Every person is necessary."

"Your group isn't going to end the war by itself." God, she sounds like Johnny.

"Someday history will record the effect we made. The results are only temporarily invisible. That's why we must keep up the pressure." His voice reverent, annoyingly preachy. "The government's policies are doomed. They can't win. In some secret room, they probably admit the truth to each other. One day, the architects of this war will be nailed for the criminals they are, you'll see. And, yeah, when I'm ready, Canada will be the easiest, cheapest place to go."

She finds herself silenced by his torrent of words. But nothing he says can promise he'll be okay. She loves Miles, but she doesn't love the bombings. It's too late to say so.

He begins stuffing the money and a few pieces of clothing into his bag, leaving her to wonder if she'll see him again.

-26-

Light from the hallway filters through the open door of the room. Paul is asleep. Since she saw him last, his pale face and the stillness of his turbulent self have stayed with her. So, too, the absence of the give-it-all-you-got husband who once sustained her. This visit will make her late for Maisie's meeting, but so be it.

He's no longer attached to lifesaving paraphernalia. The missing oxygen tank and IV drip frighten her because of what they portend.

Pulling a chair close to the bed, she lifts his cool hand to hold it in both of hers, though he doesn't respond. Perhaps he's too weak or doesn't realize that she's here. So she moves her face nearer to his and whispers words of love and forgiveness, words that come so readily they stun her.

Rushing through the cold, dark streets, she wishes she'd left Maisie's earlier. She doesn't like Sam being at home alone at night. At the meeting, the women urged her to attend the abortion-rights demonstration. She explained it was a weekday and she couldn't take off from work. But didn't say that demonstrations weren't her thing. She tried to concentrate on the plans being discussed, but the visit to Paul had upended her. She didn't mention the visit. No doubt the women would've been sympathetic and supportive, but the words she'd whispered to him of love and forgiveness would've baffled them.

As she reaches her front door, two men in overcoats appear from nowhere it seems. Their bodies stand too close to hers. She palms the front door keys.

"Celia." A low, cajoling voice, a man offering candy. "We're from the Federal Bureau of Investigation." He holds up an ID that would be difficult to see in the dark even if she bothered to look.

"It's cold out here," he says. "May we come in?"

"What do you want?" Is she even supposed to ask?

"It's about Miles. We have information. I'm sure you want to know about your son."

She switches on the weak outdoor light. The man's unlined thirtysomething face takes shape, so, too, the patent-leather blackness of his hair. Beside him, the other man remains in the dark.

Sam opens the door behind her. "Mom, who is it?"

"Go inside," she orders.

"Sam, don't you want to hear about your brother?" the man asks.

"Inside," she hisses. Sam backs away, closes the door. The man is waiting for permission to enter. She's been told what to do. "You can't come in. It's late," she says with as much certainty as she can muster.

"We'll be glad to speak with you in the morning."

"No." It's Josie's voice she's channeling now, because in truth she's curious to hear anything about Miles.

"We don't wish to inconvenience you. However, we can't talk out here."

Josie warned her that they always try to get in the house. "Speak to my lawyer."

"You're making a mistake, Celia. May I call you that?" The cajoling voice is getting on her nerves. She turns, goes inside quickly, and then closes the door gently. She can hear her own hard breathing.

Sam stares out the living room window.

"Move away from there."

"They're leaving. The car's been parked there for hours," he tells her as if she'd invited them for dinner and forgotten to cook. "What do they want?"

"To learn what they can about Miles, I guess."

"You guess? Didn't you ask?" His tone accusatory.

"It's a fishing expedition to help them catch Miles."

"He's a lot of trouble."

"He's your brother."

"So? He's still a problem." His gaze fixed on her. "Who wants these guys at our door?"

"No one. Let's go to bed, son."

"How can you ignore their visit? Don't you see the predicament Miles has put us in? He doesn't care about us, only his precious beliefs. As far as I'm concerned, he can stuff them. I don't want my life affected. He's a criminal."

"Sam, careful what you say."

"Careful what I say . . . Exactly! Before long they'll be knocking at Maria's door, and you can bet how that's going to go down with her parents."

"No one's going to call on your friend."

"You don't know that." He glares at her, and she wishes him younger, pliable, more trusting, but he's her baby no longer.

"Maria's not a member of our family. There's no reason for them to speak to her."

"Do you realize what Miles has done? This will never end."

"Sam," she pleads, placing two fingers gently on his mouth. He pushes her hand away. "Fine. I'm going to bed."

She watches him lope down the long hallway. It went badly between them. Tomorrow, she'll take him out to a diner for dinner; they'll talk again. The brothers must stick together. If the situation were reversed, Miles would support him, of that she's certain. She thinks about having a drink to try and relax, but the clock reads five past midnight.

The phone rings three times before she picks up the receiver to hear the unfamiliar, sorrowful voice. Paul is gone.

Melvin's light, even breaths rise and fall beside her as the nightly sounds of disaster escalate and retreat: police sirens, ambulances, fire trucks. The usual questions without answers bang at her brain: How long before the feds knock at her door to ask about Miles? When will she be able to finally see Richie? And what is Melvin doing that keeps him away from home for so many hours? Is it something more than taking care of Panther activities here and abroad? And then, too, how will Celia cope with Miles's situation and, now, Paul's death? These are the perilous thoughts that continue to threaten her sleep.

She could nudge Melvin awake to discuss her worries, but then they'd have to go outdoors. Anyway, it would be cruel to wake him. It's one of the few nights he's gotten to bed before three in the morning. She has to admit, though, that he has no second thoughts about waking her in the middle of the night for some loving, which can be annoying, which, come to think of it, he hasn't done in a while.

The apartment feels cold. She thinks to burrow back under the covers. Then remembers it's Saturday, glorious Saturday. No work. Melvin is out buying newspapers. In a few minutes, they'll have breakfast together. Slipping into jeans and Melvin's old sweater, she studies her face in the small magnetized mirror on the fridge. The swelling around her nose has gone down, though the bruise beneath her eye is still apparent.

Each weekend she promises herself to make order in the apartment, though too often other needs intrude. Today her plan is to find empty boxes in which to store the newspapers, leaflets, and magazines that are strewn about the place. Then she'll take dirty clothes to the Laundromat. No one in her family would live like this. Still, how often is she even at home? After work as well as on most weekends, she's out at meetings, organizing, or whatever. And she can't help but wonder if the life she's leading is her decision or a result of being her age in the here and now.

She peers into the fridge. Nothing inside will do for breakfast. Hopefully, Melvin will bring back—

There's a quick, hard rap at the door. "It's Rosemary," a serious voice calls out.

She unlocks the door. "Hi, come in. Melvin went for the papers; he'll be right back." She leads Rosemary to the kitchen table, but she's not interested in sitting.

"It's you I want to talk to," Rosemary says in an even tone she doesn't recognize.

"What's up?"

"Here's what we need you to know. We in the party like you and respect the work you do. But Melvin is a leader in the struggle, a Black leader who shouldn't be living with a white woman. It sends the wrong message not only to Black sisters but also to the struggle. It's how the party feels. Nothing personal, Josie, understand?"

She stares at Rosemary's expressive eyes, her brown satin skin, the close-cropped black hair and long silver earrings that brush the shoulders of her leather jacket. Hears Melvin's keys unlock the door, sees him deposit a paper bag and newspapers on the table.

"Hey, sister, what's happening?"

"I came to speak to Josie and I did." Rosemary's voice is low.

"If this is a woman thing, I'll disappear, but if it's about me, sister, don't waste Josie's ears. I don't want her bothered. Understand? Anything to share, I'm listening." He smiles, though his eyes are blazing.

"You know why I came, Melvin. See you at the office. No offense, Josie. Take care." And she's out the door.

"I'm sorry," he mumbles on his way to shower.

She empties the bag—half dozen eggs and loaf of rye. Finding a bowl, she breaks four eggs, adds spices, while Rosemary's words repeat in her head: "You know why I came, Melvin."

As she beats the eggs, a woman making breakfast for her lover, her soul mate, a blizzard of questions assails her. Why did she remain mute? Why didn't she tell Rosemary that she wouldn't accept backward requests no matter where they originated? No revolution is damaged by love, she could've said that. Why not challenge the party, ask that they analyze what good could come from their request? She and Melvin together are more than the color of their skin. They're comrades, repositories of many experiences. Why didn't she assert as much? Or make a million other rejoinders? No one would accuse her of being shy. What stopped her?

His body still damp from the shower, he dresses quickly. She watches his long muscular legs disappear into pants, dark arms slide into a white shirt, the contrast suddenly blinding.

"Don't let the sister's words upset you, the visit most unfortunate," he mutters. "Okay, girl? Listen, I have to take care of something. See you later." He grabs his jacket and is out the door faster than she can think what to say.

A sense of numbness rises to still her. Is he on his way to scream bloody murder at Panther women for their interference? Or will he avoid the office and the criticism-self-criticism session that's bound to occur there? Wherever he's headed, it won't include her. Whatever is discussed, he won't tell her. It's better that way. Having to defend herself for being a handicap to the struggle . . . it's too awful to consider.

Strangely, she isn't pissed at Rosemary. It must've been tough to be the one to inform her. They've been friends. Melvin has told her that the party believes carrying out difficult tasks helps members develop a hard skin in the face of adversity. But it feels mean.

The beaten eggs, like flayed flesh, repel her. She flushes them down the toilet. Then sits at the desk, an old door thrown across two police barricades they "borrowed" one summer evening after a demonstration. Glancing out the shadeless window at the uncaring sky, she makes a list in her head of what needs to be accomplished today, beginning with the Laundromat.

Melvin's been at home more than five minutes but hasn't yet spoken. Her eyes follow his movements for any hint of what's to come. The cold dark sky is lit by a full moon.

He fills the old kettle with water, rinses out two cups, places them on the table, spoons in instant coffee, then when the water boils, fills each cup.

"Let's have coffee."

They sit at the table facing each other.

"I wish this morning didn't happen, Josie." The streetlights paint the wall a sad yellow.

"Me too."

"I wanted to bring up the issue weeks ago but couldn't figure out how to deal with such a hard task. I've been walking the avenues, but there's no good way, none at all." Words slip from his too-familiar lips. Nothing complicated here, yet her ability to absorb is greatly impaired. "Thing is . . . this is a racist system. You know that, girl, right? Say you know it."

"I know it's so."

"Other thing is, the party is right, though I resent the interference. Present conditions, that is, this racist country, make living with a white woman a problem." No hand slides across to reassure hers.

"You want to leave because I'm white?" Her words so soft she wonders if he hears them.

"That's a misrepresentation."

She gazes at his earnest expression but won't modify her statement.

"It's about the struggle. You know that." He stares at his coffee cup as if the script is written there.

"Isn't it Stalinist to do whatever the party says no matter what?"

"I don't give a shit what the party says." And his eyes log her face. "It's what I believe that counts."

"You're making a terrible mistake."

A flicker of doubt or maybe annoyance crosses his face. "We're not talking choices or personal preferences. We're talking how to do all that's necessary to make ourselves available to the historical moment."

"What does history have to do with our life together?"

"Black people are in the vanguard of the struggle. Everything we do is noticed, counted, reflected upon, judged, see? It would give the Man great pleasure to destroy us, not just the party, but also any Black rebel. They'll use whatever ruse they can. A Black man with a white woman is grist for their mill."

"Why give in to their racism?" Because isn't that the crux of the matter?

"It's timing, Josie, timing. What we do today, tomorrow, makes another scene possible later."

"You've said this before. What's different now?" She's struggling to keep her voice above a whisper.

"I'll be traveling. A lot. In addition to international prospects, we're opening party offices in the South. Actually I'm about to leave to organize college students in North Carolina, Alabama, and Mississippi to help run these offices. If we achieve national representation, young blacks will flock to us."

The ceiling light shines on his face as if he's on a stage. It's Melvin, her Melvin, the man who held her all night after her father died, who washed away the blood from her beating. "How can you use politics to make decisions about our relationship?"

"Everything is political; it's what fuels the struggle, helps us evaluate next steps instead of bowing to old ways of thinking."

She's trying, really she is, to take in his every word, but nothing adheres.

"Those who rule this country preach, teach, and insist on American individualism. They exalt the few who pull themselves up by their bootstraps, neglecting to say how many millions still walk barefoot."

His sudden intensity, the quick frown. He's found a cogent point of view and it energizes him.

"Look at the important work that you're doing to organize white people," he continues. "You're trying to change racist thinking. You're trying to create a different kind of thinking, marchers against the war, women fighters. You're trying to make it happen here and now, and it's what you should be doing. It's where you should be doing it, not with me living in some rural Black area."

"What if the people in the South don't agree with your plans? What if they aren't ready? How do you know it's time—"

"Are you saying Black people should wait? That the time isn't ripe to insist on our rights, fight for our freedom, and do whatever's necessary? Because if that's what you're implying, you're dead wrong. Black people are stirred now and want to take action. History offers few spontaneous moments, and this is one of them."

"And you're an agent of history?"

"The party is ready to consolidate and translate rural needs into action. In addition to breakfast programs, we'll squat on the land and carry out other operations suitable to the people living there." His patient tone indicates he's prepared to go on, convince, reiterate. "And living with a white woman invites trouble, especially down there, and distracts from our fight for liberation."

"Liberation?" she repeats as if she's never heard the word before, because other words, "betrayal," "treachery," "breach," run in a headline around her brain. Her muscles tighten as if by a screwdriver.

"Yeah, baby. To achieve it we have to bring together Blacks

in the North and South, solidify ties with Africa, and make a mountain out of a minority. Confronting this racist society will take all of that and more, and I know you know that too. Right now we must buy Black, live Black, and love Black."

This is the conversation she never wanted to have, the one she can't win.

"My people's needs are my priority, my reality. I must abide by that. Do you hear what I'm saying?"

You're my heart is the lyric in her head.

"Can you understand, girl?"

The Vietnamese woman, rifle in hand, infant on her back, stares out of the wall poster with sudden indifference. "I don't. I can't."

"Baby, you think it's easy for me?" He leans toward her with troubled eyes. "It's hard for both of us. I know that. You got to know that too. But the revolution comes first, before me, before you, before any particular individual. Otherwise we can't succeed. Malcolm, Martin, Fred. How many others have already given their lives to the struggle? Didn't they have lovers, children, parents?" His tone a plea, his face drawn, shoulders sagging beneath the weight of his tasks.

For a weird second, she wants to console him, afraid he's offering up his life. And she tries to see past his words to the core of him, where her trust dwells, but a painful weariness wraps itself around her. Appeal, lament, argue against his arguments, she could do that. But even if she found a way— miraculously—to change his mind and keep him here, would it be the same?

The poster of Ho Chi Minh sitting on a log exudes tolerance, tenacity, wisdom.

"Baby, we've had great years together."

"Had?" she says softly. The distance between them widening like an oil spill. But still their clothing rests together on chairs, their shoes under the bed, their books on the floor, his pillow near hers. The room is cold, but her cheeks are hot, feverish.

"Josie, please, I need you to understand."

He needs her to agree so he can leave without guilt. She can't agree. She won't.

His eyes remain steady on her. What does he see? Is she crumbling? She's upright in the chair, no tears. Two hands in her lap, her hammering heart loud but personal. Weird pressure squeezes her brain, and her frozen body is burning, but how would he know? Still, he waits for a response, the one he wants.

"Love never damaged a revolution" is all she can muster.

"I'll always love you, girl. You must know that." He's out of the chair, pulling her to her feet. He wraps his arms tight around her, his lips on hers so urgent this must be the final nourishment.

"Not sorry about us, ever, no," he mumbles. "You take care, girl," he whispers. Then he closes the door behind him so softly she barely hears it. But the sound of the locks, one, two, three, is loud and clear.

Knife-edged light pries open her eyes. Sun glazes the wall as filigreed shadows slink across the bed. The phone rings. Her neck feels stiff, her arms useless, and her legs leaden beneath the crumpled sheet. Car horns, rumbling trucks, the phone still ringing, steam pipes banging, though heat rarely arrives. A neighbor flushes a toilet, a middle-of-the-night sound, but it's daytime. Why is the overhead light still on? Melvin is gone. He's not coming back. The phone continues to ring. She covers her ears but hears it anyway and lifts and replaces the receiver; the ringing stops.

Once, when she was little, she woke from a nightmare to discover a horrid huge roach crossing her chest; she screamed. Her father came running in, told her she'd been dreaming, that there was nothing there, and that everything was okay. No one can tell her that now. The nightmare is real. Melvin is gone; he's not coming back. The phone rings again. She lifts the receiver intending to keep it off the hook but hears Maisie's voice.

"Where are you? We're waiting."

"Melvin's gone." The words an incantation.

"What?" Maisie's incredulous tone doesn't help.

"Left last night. Finished between us."

"Why?"

"Because he's Black, I'm white, and the world won't have it."

"We'll come to your place after the action."

"No. I need sleep, not talk." She replaces the receiver.

Pulling the blanket up over her head in search of oblivion, her too-awake brain won't comply. Her mind combs through the last weeks, last days, for signs she must've ignored or rationalized. How could he extinguish love like a candle? How could his words about how special things were between them, how lucky they were to have each other, become worthless? How could the struggle to create a more just society lead to such misery? Revolution? He left her for the revolution? How dare he leave her for an idea?

She never did go to the Laundromat. Her eyes take in the usual clutter, dirty clothes in a pile, posters, newspapers; nothing has changed, and how can that be? Where are her tears? She's in pain. She doesn't want to go through this. There must be another way. People can deny or forget anything. What exactly does she want to forget? That he left, that he was ever here, that she's expected to go on? Go on with what? The minutia of daily life, leaflets, meetings, and demonstrations? Why should she? What's the point? In the end it is personal, isn't it, God damn it to hell, all of it? Why did she never buy a shade to lock out the sun so she could pretend it's night? Only sleep can insulate her. Somewhere she read that when roused from a coma, a person can experience the past differently. But it didn't say how to induce one.

The banging at the door wakes her. If she says nothing, maybe it will stop.

"Josie, let me in."

The ceiling light still blazes, but outside now, the blue haze of dusk. She wants only more sleep. Her head feels hot and achy. A fever that will spike and land her in a hospital where someone will get word to Melvin, and . . . Pathetic. Did Che's wife suffer when he took off to Bolivia? Did she feel abandoned? Did Che even discuss it with her? Or did the New Man leave his woman the way men have left for eons?

"Josie, I heard about you and Melvin," Ben calls loudly.

Even if she doesn't respond, he won't go away, but the neighbors will get an earful. Slipping off the bed, she finds Melvin's T-shirt coiled like a snake on the floor, pulls it on, finds her way to the door, unlocks it, and heads back to bed.

"Maisie told me that Melvin left because of the struggle. Is that a fair description?" Ben perches on the side of the bed, Melvin's side.

"Fair?" She laughs and it's a harsh sound. "What's fair about one person deciding about two people's lives? What the fuck's fair about that, Ben?"

"I'm here to help you." His denim work shirt offers the stale smell of weed.

Her mind entertains the word "help," but it's not good enough, holds no promise. If he can't offer her at least one of three magical wishes, there's little he can do to help. "Don't believe you can do that."

"Let me do . . ." He stretches out beside her. The shadow of a beard darkens his cheeks, his curly hair a halo around his head; maybe he is an angel.

"Do what, exactly? Sex? The cure-all, end-all, be-all, of healing, the culmination of every male-female dilemma?"

"I bring only comfort." His tone gentle, his usual merry eyes worried or maybe just sad for her.

She averts her head to hide the sudden tears and stares at the varied cracks in the wall, which she and Melvin used to interpret. He saw famous black faces. She described wild sex scenes, which made him laugh.

"It's a bad patch. You'll see."

"See what, Ben?"

"That you'll heal, get back to yourself."

"Don't want to."

"What does that mean?"

"Too complicated to explain, too tired to talk. I need to sleep."

"What's complicated? You've been ditched. It happens to all of us. Love comes again, believe me."

Maybe . . . for others, but she doesn't want it to come again with someone else, doesn't subscribe to the cliché "Better to have loved and lost"; how could it be better? Her perspective has been turned inside out, her ability to trust eroded, and her sense of security been shot to hell. Love another man? Why would she dare? Ditched for the revolution . . . Our love, our relationship, an impediment to meeting the needs of the people?

"It hurts, but Melvin is a Black man who—"

"Oh, spare me. I can't hear it again."

"Why else would he leave? You've been happy together for years," Ben says.

"Maybe I missed the clues."

"Do you believe him?"

She doesn't answer.

"The Black struggle is heating up. He is a leader. So go with the facts."

"What makes you suddenly wise?"

"Probably the dope I smoke." His tone still gentle.

She gazes at the poster-filled walls.

He slips off the bed. "I'm about to serve tea for two."

"Ben, stop. I can't drink anything; sleep is all."

He gazes at her. "Then give me a set of keys so I can check on you."

"How come you're not high?" He's rarely this serious.

"I'm about to amend that when I leave here."

"In the top drawer, an extra set." She watches him pocket the keys, open and close the door. Yes, she thinks, of course Melvin left for the struggle and for no other reason. What hurts is that he did so without her.

-28-

Celia trudges across the opalescent, snow-pocked beach holding the box in front of her like a gift. Inside is bone and gristle that could belong to anyone. Last night in her bedroom she studied the contents, thinking to say a prayerful word or two, but it felt too weird speaking to a heap of shavings. In bed, though, she stared at the empty place that Paul had once occupied, and his absence became palpable. It was as if he'd just been beside her and then whisked away.

When her father died, her mother murmured that it was the proper order of things, parents before children, but what about husbands and wives?

At yesterday's brief service for Paul, the few people who attended shed no tears. Still, for her, it was more rending than she'd anticipated. Suddenly she missed him terribly again. When he was gone from her life while still alive, she banished him from her mind. Now that he's dead, she's more than reluctant to let him go. That he loved her was never in dispute for either one of them. Knowing this may steady her. Their years together happened. She owns them. He left her their sons. She's grateful for that.

She glances at them now: Sam's head is down staring at the sand, and Quince wears an expression she can't decode. A while back, Quince said his father was a coward for leaving them. Yet it was Quince who contacted hospitals and ERs to find Paul.

Miles should be here. Without him the ritual feels incomplete. Neither son asks about their brother. Strangely enough, Johnny asked if he should try and find Miles. She told him no, let it be.

Her mother's head and shoulders are wrapped in scarves against the cold; the family has folded her within its small circle. Terry's slim body shivers in a mini-length coat, her cheeks red and raw. Johnny talks to the priest, a friend he convinced to participate. Josie would've been here if she weren't at home sick. So, too, Richie if he were stateside. Her women's group stands a little apart from the family. Clustered near them are Paul's bandmates, whom she hasn't spoken to in months. Who told them?

Snowflakes drift out of a pewter sky to land in the dense black water.

As the priest finishes reading the psalm, the wind picks up the muttered "Amens."

Quince says, "Mom, we're ready. We'll each take a handful and toss it in the ocean. I'll go first, then Sam, then you. Okay?" She nods. All of her sons have Paul's eyes.

Her gloved fingers grip the box so tightly someone else will have to prize open the lid.

"Here, let me." Johnny takes the box from her.

"Go on then," she urges Quince once the box is open.

Quince takes a fistful of ashes, then walks carefully to the water, a tall boy with a straight back. He tosses the ashes, which the wind picks up and deposits on the sand.

Sam dips into the box, then jogs to the water. With a rapid overhand motion, he pitches the ashes as if they were too hot to handle. Once more the wind lifts and scatters them along the beach.

Johnny is saying, "Celia, your turn."

Roper begins to play the sax. She hears the varied tones as wails of protest: Not yet, my lady, not yet.

Pulling off her gloves, she takes a fistful of ashes in each hand. "One for Miles," she says aloud. Someday she will tell him how he was present in his absence. With her eyes steady on the bruised horizon, she walks until the toes of her boots are in the white wake.

"This one from Miles," she whispers. "And this from me." Then lets go of both handfuls. The wind blows the ashes back in her face. A faint smile cracks her frozen cheeks. So like Paul, recalcitrant to the end.

She searches for Quince through the gritty windows of the slowly departing train taking him back to West Point. He didn't want her to see him off, but she insisted, can't get enough of each of them as they grow up and leave her. As the last car pulls out of the station, the train lights up the tunnel for an instant before the long throat of darkness returns.

She heads out into the cold street. Shoulders hunched against the wind, she walks uptown. She isn't ready to go home.

She rings the bell. "Josie, it's me, Celia."

"A minute," a muffled voice says.

In a grubby long T-shirt, Josie opens the door, her face pale, drawn.

"Sorry about Paul; sorry I couldn't be there to say good-bye."

Celia touches her sister's forehead. "Warm. Go back to bed."

The apartment smells like curdled milk. No surprise. An uncapped milk container has been left out on the table. She pours it down the drain, then runs the water. She won't ask how long it's been since Josie cleaned, but getting down on one knee, she's about to wipe up a spill.

"Celia, stop cleaning." Josie sits in bed, the blanket thrown to one side.

"Order will help."

"No. It won't."

"Maisie told me that your boyfriend left. How are you?" Celia pulls a chair to the foot of the bed.

"Is there a trick to deleting misery?"

"Just go through it," she says, knowing the pitfalls of the journey.

"Like there's a magical light at the end of the—"

"No light, Josie, but it's the only way to reach the other side."

"Are you on the other side of it?"

In Josie's voice she hears her own grief. It may have been a mistake coming here so soon after scattering Paul's ashes.

"Are you?" Josie probes.

"After Paul walked out, I was too angry to think straight. Then I refused to think about him at all. And then he died, which has made it difficult all over again. Yesterday, on the beach, when Roper blew the sax, it was Paul playing, except it wasn't and never would be again."

"He died a little when they stopped appreciating his music," Josie says.

"True. Yesterday was also sad because Miles wasn't there."

Josie's face registers only her own unhappiness.

"You won't always be this miserable. Not because time heals, but life insists on itself and you go on; you just do, Josie."

"I want to believe you."

"The women's group helped me some," she says. "Though my

past and theirs isn't at all alike, when it came to broken relationships, the similarities were illuminating. And so what? you might ask. Well, every woman in the group had gone through some form of loss or breakup, though reasons might differ. It became clear to me that each woman ended up being okay and that was encouraging."

"Melvin left to meet the needs of his people."

"I don't understand all the ins and outs of his struggle. I do understand that it's simply unbearable to lose someone you love, and when it happens no reasons are ever good enough."

"His presence is still palpable. When it got dark and lamp-light brightened the room, our shadows used to cross the wall together. It's as if each piece of furniture mocks his absence."

Celia gazes at her little sister, who has been a grown-up far longer than she realized. "When the fever is gone, come stay with me for a while. And visit Ma. I know Ma and Johnny don't understand the life you lead. But they love you."

"I fear that if I step into their vortex, I'll never be free again."

"Well, that's simply not true. You have a life. It's yours, not theirs. I should get home. Though, lately, Sam has been hanging out at his friend Maria's house until dark."

"Any word about Richie?"

"Ma received a letter two days ago. He's being shipped state-side to be mustered out and then will be sent home. It won't be long now. We decided he would live with me for a while. I have the extra room. He'll want to see you. I'd like to have a welcome-home party."

"Oh Jesus, Celia, don't. It's the last thing he'll want."

"Are you sure?"

"Positive. It's horrid to be backslapped by family and friends for something you can't come to grips with."

"Oh, I see. I'm glad you told me. Could I heat up some soup for you before I leave?"

"Please don't."

"You should consider joining my women's group," she says, slipping into her coat.

Watching her sister leave, she thinks to get out of bed and lock the door but doesn't. With Melvin gone and Miles heaven knows where, danger feels further away than just outside her door. She's discouraged friends from visiting. Even Ben, who has a key, she shoos away soon after he appears. Doesn't want to talk about Melvin, doesn't want to either blame or defend him to any of them. Doesn't want to think about him at all.

Switching on the TV, she finds a rerun of an old movie, which will lull her to sleep the way it has each afternoon of the past week.

Someone knocks hard at the door. Outside the window, only blueberry darkness. It's late.

"Who's there?"

"Johnny."

She slips into jeans and unlocks the door. "Celia was here a few hours ago." It sounds like an accusation.

"Oh yeah?" His grim expression registers the mess of her. He's not in uniform and totes a shopping bag in each hand. He walks past her to the kitchen table. "Ma cooked; Terry packed. Have you seen the doctor?"

"No. It's just a virus or the flu. My boyfriend isn't living here anymore. His departure didn't help my condition."

"You have a boyfriend?"

"Yes, a fighter in the liberation struggle. He had to leave because he needs to help his people. He's Black." Swallowing against the pressure of tears, she scans her brother's face. He looks perplexed, uncomfortable, and for a moment she feels sorry for him.

"Johnny, I'm tired of lying is all." She is, bone tired of storing truths in different boxes, each with its own lock and key, each labeled appropriately, tired of having to figure out which one to open where and with whom.

He waits for her to say more. When she doesn't, he begins to unpack the bags.

"Ma wants the empty containers returned. I have to go. I'm on duty in an hour." He eyes the three locks before opening the door. "I'm glad it's not pneumonia."

Instructions are written on each container: *Store on second fridge shelf. Cook at 350. Broil only. Keep in freezer. Discard after 5 days.*

She waves good-bye to one of the nurses and heads out of the hospital. Back at work a few weeks now, she still finds it easier to share pleasantries than any truth about her life. Her job is more interesting since she was promoted a while ago to work with hospital case managers. She's learning a bit about medicine. Twice she's been allowed to follow midwives making rounds in the maternity ward. Her supervisor has floated the possibility of a hospital-paid fellowship in midwifery. She hasn't responded. She isn't sure.

The evenings are lighter longer, and gloves remain stuffed in her pocket. People rush past, eager to get home. It's where she'd like to go instead of to the corner bar. Nina phoned at work, said meeting was imperative. Thing is, she has no wish to be filled in on what's happening politically. She said as much to Ben the other night when he phoned. Several times now, he's offered to escort her on any outing of her choice. What that could possibly be, she hasn't a clue.

The bar is crowded and noisy with hospital staff coming off shift, many still in scrubs. It's hot inside and the rancid mixture of beer and cigarettes doesn't help. Both TVs are broadcasting the news of endless war, but no one seems to be watching, including her.

In the dim light, she spots Nina and Maisie at a table in the rear.

"Shall I pour?" Maisie asks, lifting a pitcher of beer.

"Not for me," Josie says.

Nina studies her. "You still look a little drawn but otherwise okay."

"That's a relief."

Maisie slides an arm around her shoulders. "You haven't let us say anything about Melvin leaving. It's difficult because he's someone we all admire. But here goes . . . You've been robbed of every woman's right to shout, 'Bastard,' 'Scumbag,' and 'Worthless piece of trash,' because he's not. However, he didn't prepare you for his decision. If by any chance you're blaming yourself, which women do all the time, stop. And you're wrong if you believe that if you'd done such instead of other such, the relationship could've been saved. Point is men don't go through the same process."

"Why not?" Nina asks.

"A patriarchal society teaches men they're too important to waste energy on emotions. Also their relationship to love is strange. I haven't figured it out yet."

"Listen, I'm tired," Josie says. "I really want to get home."

Nina slides a cool hand over hers. "We're in the initial stages of plotting something big, a women's march on the Pentagon to coincide with the Vietnam vets who plan to throw away their medals. It won't happen for a while, but it's a necessary response to the everyday atrocities."

"Women in several states have already committed to work on it. And men could attend but women would lead it," Maisie says and begins to list the reasons why it's such an important action.

She half listens, thinking Maisie is wrong. She doesn't blame herself for Melvin's leaving.

"And you, Josie, are the perfect woman to be its prime organizer."

She gazes at her friends' hopeful expressions. "Thanks for the vote of confidence. But my political beliefs are floating around unattached to me. It's a great action. It really is. But I want no part of the intensity." On her friends' faces, she reads, Isn't it time to return to the self she was before Melvin left? Hasn't everyone allowed her the requisite number of days to recover? The answer is yes, but it doesn't change her response.

"Josie, you can't keep hiding. You have to try to jump back in. It's the only way to heal." Nina's tone unusually soft.

"I won't be told it's the only way to heal. Can I go home now?" Tears press at her eyelids.

Entering the apartment, she sees at once that Melvin's shoes are no longer near the bed. When she checks, his clothes are gone from the closet as well. That he took only what was his and nothing that they owned together isn't a surprise. She knew that one day he'd return for his things but didn't imagine it would be today.

PART THREE

-30-

Celia is greeted by the usual rows of bent heads and buzz of sewing machines as a watery sun illuminates the ancient factory walls. She waves to Denise, who returns the gesture with a nod. Her friend feels neglected. She explained that her women's group takes up more of her free time now, but Denise wasn't impressed.

Her boss is in his office. She reminds herself it's now or never. How difficult could it be? Is it the fear of change? Paul would say, Do it, of course he would. Miles would too, definitely, if only she could ask him. Oh, she must stop going at herself like this.

She taps at the glass of his cage. Without looking up, Artie beckons her in. He's behind a gray metal desk, rifling through invoices. Dressed as always in T-shirt and jeans, he continues doing whatever he's doing. He won't say anything until she does.

"I have something to tell you."

"You're pregnant?"

"Artie, that's awful."

"Why? You're young, healthy, so what's wrong?" He shuts a ledger, leans back in his chair.

"Women are more than reproductive equipment."

"Of course. Just being silly. What is it, Celia?"

"I'm giving you two weeks' notice." There, she said it.

He sits up and the chair snaps forward. "Is this a joke?"

"No joke."

"Why? You haven't had to do overtime in months. What happened?"

"My friend has opened a food co-op. She asked me to become a buyer and to help coordinate everything at a decent salary."

"How much more money than here?"

"It's not the wages. It's time to do something different." She mimics the words of the women in her group, one of whom will be her new boss, though none speak of bosses, only collectives.

He looks bewildered. "What if it doesn't work out? What if you don't like it? What if they go broke?"

She's already asked herself these questions. But Artie is waiting for an answer. "I'm turning forty. I have to risk something."

"Who says so? Where's it written? There's nothing magic in the number. I've been there for three years and still put my pants on the same way."

"Doing something different, meeting new people, what's wrong with that?" Does she really expect Artie to tell her?

"You've been through hell, losing Paul, and then Miles disappearing God knows where. We're your friends, we care, and here everyone knows your name."

"I care about everyone here too."

"Even me?" His voice drops.

"What a silly question."

"Vi and I separated."

"I'm sorry."

He shrugs. Once more he leans back in his chair. "So, okay, listen. Go. Try the new venture. I won't hire anyone for two weeks after you leave. If it doesn't work out, come back. If it does, I'll phone you. There's a great steak house near Yankee Stadium. It has sawdust on the floor, and the waiters are at least ninety years old, but the food, it's glorious."

At her machine, as ribbons of silk slide through her fingers, she ponders the last minutes. So he wants to date her? It's not as if she has to ask anyone's permission.

Headed toward the bus stop, she reminds herself that the factory schedule will be replaced by another schedule, so it's not as if she's going into some job of ease. Actually, she was told it would be busier but would feel less like a harness. When she shared the job change with her family, they reacted as Josie had predicted, unhappily. To them, and to some extent to her as well, unnecessary change is dangerous. Josie, though, had championed the idea, said it was a good way to go forward.

It does feel right, maybe even exciting, to do something more daring. Miles would be proud if he knew, she's certain. If only someone could assure her that he was safe, she could enjoy the moment more. An attorney did brief her on how to respond when the FBI visits again.

The streets that crisscross Third Avenue are always crowded. The El trains screech and groan and interrupt serious conversations. Cars pile up at every light, and nothing gives way whatever the time of day. It's a major Bronx shopping area, with department stores that sell cheap clothing. Customers can buy now and pay later. Several of the women at work have bought dresses, worn them, and then returned them tags and all.

At the bus stop, it occurs to her that the usual reasons to hurry home are melting away like soap bubbles. Sam now has a part-time job after school and often has dinner at Maria's. It does feel luxurious to enter an empty house where no one needs her immediate attention. Tonight, she'll pour herself a glass of wine, toast her newfound courage, and then phone Josie with the news.

The steak house near Yankee Stadium definitely sounds like an interesting place in which to dine out.

Heading to Celia's place, she does her best not to anticipate, prepare, or expect. What? She doesn't know, which is nerve-racking. Surprises and the like are not her thing. Too often, they're negative: so-and-so died, lost their job, or whatever. It made her feel helpless.

The familiar two-story brick houses seem older than ever with their chipped eaves and cluttered gutters. Though Christmas is long past, a few wreaths still hang on doors. It's almost noon but many windows have their blinds drawn. Aimless thoughts to still her anxious heart.

The bedroom door is ajar. A wispy cloud of smoke hangs below the ceiling light. Richie sits in an armchair beside the window.

"Hey." Tears clog her throat.

"Hey, Sister Josie," he offers without emotion.

She kisses his warm cheek, sees his trembling hand clutch the chair arm, an ashtray and lighter on the sill. He's in jeans and an oversize black sweater, his hair shorter than it's ever been. His large dark eyes refuse her reflection.

She perches on the bottom bunk bed, where for years she and Miles read, talked, and horsed around.

"How are you?" she asks.

"Okay, and you?"

"The answer is relative."

He says nothing.

"Did you receive my letters while in the hospital?"

"Yeah, thanks."

"Celia's at the co-op?"

He nods.

"Has Ma visited?"

"Last evening. She brought dinner but didn't stay."

"Anyone else come by?

"Johnny came with a six-pack, hung out briefly. We didn't talk, not much to say."

She wants to hug him tightly but senses it wouldn't be appreciated.

"Did Celia tell you that Melvin took off? That he needs to dedicate himself to the struggle?"

He stubs out the butt of his cigarette, pulls another from the pack with his lips, then reaches for the lighter with his steady hand. "He seemed a devoted guy."

"Yeah, he was till he wasn't."

Silence.

"Is there anything you need?"

He looks at her.

"I mean at the store."

He shakes his head.

Silence.

There's so much she wants to know: Is he disappointed to be home? Would he actually have re-upped? Does his body hurt? Does he do anything except sit here? "Richie, how should I talk to you? What's taboo? What's okay? Give me a clue. Tell me not to ask questions and I won't. Tell me you need silence, and I'll not utter a sound, but tell me. I missed you *so* much." Again, tears threaten.

"I freak everyone out, even myself. The grease that eases words is gone, so talking's a jolt. There's no familiar. I manage to wait till the afternoon to start drinking. Then who cares?"

"Maybe you should talk to other vets."

"Maybe I will. Probably I won't. Numbness is bliss, and it's what I aim for."

He lifts one arm with the other and lowers it onto his lap, where it moves of its own volition.

"Can you dress yourself?"

"It takes a while, eating too, yeah, but walking . . . Ever watch a two-year-old cross a room? Get us some beers, Josie, will you? There's a bunch in the fridge."

Outside the kitchen window, an empty gray street of look-alike houses. It could've been worse, she repeats to herself, the words she heard growing up. Only death was accepted as the worst. And he's alive and home. Isn't that enough? But his spirit is gone, sucked out of him. She's seen it with other vets: alone with nightmares, unable to give voice to the ravages of experience. No wonder conversation is difficult. Of all her siblings, Richie was the most joyful, danced around rooms and laughed easily. It took a lot to get him down, and even then, he didn't linger there.

She remembers his long phone calls with girlfriends, the mess of a car he careened around in, the radio blasting. The beach, she remembers that too, the heat mixed with the smell of baby lotion. The sandy blankets crowded with friends vying for Richie's attention. He never minded that she was there.

The high hopes he left with, his dreams of travel, adventure, how he would use the military to fulfill them, she can't forget that either. He was funny, sweet, sexy, and always someone in the know and nothing like the somber, pale man in that room.

Seeing Richie this way brings the war up close and heart-stoppingly personal. Her friends are right. Thousands of people must show up and bang open the Pentagon doors to overwhelm the officials there and be heard. She'll do what she can and be there with them; of course she will.

On the refrigerator door, tiny magnets hold photos of grand-parents, parents, children, siblings, aunts, uncles, cousins. Her family writ large, staring back at her, wanting to know: What is she doing living alone and grieving for a relationship that won't happen?

Snatching a few beers from the fridge, she rushes back to the bedroom. For the first time in weeks, her energy flows like a storm-driven river. She kneels beside her brother. "Richie, I'm going to find us a two-bedroom apartment in Manhattan. With a cane, you'll soon be able to walk to a nearby movie, bar, whatever. It's the boonies here. Stuck inside, it's awful. Say yes, please."

-32-

Walking through the small unadorned lobby, she revels in her achievement. It took less than a week to find the right apartment: two bedrooms, ground floor, in an old prewar building on Seventy-Fifth Street, on the corner of Broadway. With her paycheck and Richie's disability money, they'll be able to swing the rent and then some.

Ben borrowed a truck to move stuff here. They arranged the furniture for Richie's convenience. There's only one conventional lock on the door, not three locks. None of the posters from her other apartment are hung on the wall, though she told her friends she'd help organize the Pentagon action.

The new place doesn't feel like home yet. An aura of spookiness prevails, like the feeling of finding oneself the only person in a movie theatre. Surely it will become more homey next week after Richie moves in. Then her friends will visit; so will her sister and even Grace and Carla. Maybe even one or two of Richie's vet friends. He must have some. She's trying to be hopeful. A new apartment doesn't mean starting over, of course not. What does it mean? She hasn't figured that out. When she signed the lease, it occurred to her that Melvin would no longer know her address. She's able to let that happen, which is courage of a sort.

The phone wakes her from a scary dream she doesn't want to remember. Faint light filters through the window. Not quite awake, she lifts the receiver. "Hello."

"Josie, it's Ben. Not good news." She listens as he unfolds the tale.

"I have to call Celia." It's early but her sister needs to know. First she needs to gather her thoughts, her strength. But her thoughts frighten her.

Celia picks up on the first ring. "I know. I heard last night. The attorney phoned me." She speaks quickly as if ready to rush out the door.

"Which attorney?" Josie asks.

"Don Watts. Is he very young? I want a white-haired, stoop-shouldered man to be at my son's side like a father."

"It doesn't matter; he's part of a legal team. What did he say?"

"They have scant evidence to tie Miles to anything but the last action, which didn't happen. I'll be able to see him briefly after the arraignment."

"I want to see him too."

"Don said we have to be careful. They'll log his visits. You're an activist. It may not be helpful."

She wants to argue this but lets it go. "Did the attorney say anything about a plea?"

"Miles and the others will plead not guilty with extenuating circumstances, which Don says would offer a historical context to what he's accused of. He doubted there'd be bail set, because they're fugitives."

"Oh, Celia, I'm so sad, so sorry, so—"

"Something else," Celia says. "Sam stayed awake with me all night, though he didn't talk much. He decided to go to school this morning. It's baffling."

"He can't handle it is why. What about you?"

"All night I could hear Paul cautioning me to stay loose, but I'm terrified. What's worse is that it's out of my hands. I have to rely on others. No one I know, no one who loves Miles as much as I do."

"Oh, Celia, I'm so sorry. Where's Richie?"

"He takes a heavy dose of something to help him sleep. I haven't told him yet. I need to get dressed."

Josie replaces the receiver, feeling that she let her sister down, but what could she say? That unless there's a miracle, the only question now is how long the sentence will be and where Miles will be sent? Though she ought to get ready for work, she can't perform normal but can't remain here either, where suddenly the bare walls feel threatening.

She phones Ben.

"It's me. Are you busy?"

"When?"

"Now. Later too?"

"I had a temporary gig at some library, but I was hoping for someone to dissuade me. So, yes, I mean, no, I'm not busy. What do you need?"

"I don't know."

"Okay. Do you want me to bring breakfast?"

"No. Can I come to your place?"

"I'm waiting. And, Josie, we'll face it. Miles belongs to all of us."

As she walks up Amsterdam Avenue to Ben's place, her mind juggles different possibilities for Miles, but none promise anything other than prison. Escaping would be the only way out, and how in hell would he be able to do that? When they were little and made up various games, Miles favored one, not exactly hide-and-seek, but almost. She was to be kidnapped and taken somewhere far away and hard to find, but he would search until he found her. Sometimes she'd hide in one of the nearby stores or in a distant telephone booth. He was always able to find and free her. Now he'll be whisked away to God knows where. And what in heavens can she do to free him?

She passes a tall, elegant building of expensive apartments, where a uniformed doorman stands beneath a canopy as glass doors slide open and closed. She wonders if any of the people living there protest the war, racism, or sexism. Or do they pursue their daily lives as if none of it is happening? To them, the arrest of Miles would mean nothing. Yet in her old neighborhood, Miles's arrest will be a tale that will travel from one mouth to another like all good stories. Not because they know him or care about how it will resolve but because troubles elsewhere can offer temporary soothing. In the end, it will be her family that will be left to deal with the story's outcome. Maybe some things never leave home.

Ben's studio apartment is indecently neat. On his walls are the posters missing from hers. In the two-by-four kitchen, he beats eggs for omelets. Beside him, she fills the coffeepot, then pops bread in the toaster. Music she doesn't recognize is playing softly.

"I thought about offering you some dope, but . . . I don't know. . ."

"Too early for drugs, too late for Miles," she says. "You realize nothing short of a miracle will keep him from prison."

"I realize."

"My sister's there now, waiting to see him. The lawyers want me to stay away, call me an activist like it's a bad thing."

"You'll see him soon enough. In truth, Josie, you can't offer him anything helpful right now. I talked to one of the members of the legal team last night. He thinks, given the antiwar movement and the historical moment, that extenuating circumstances may have an effect on the outcome."

"Like what?"

"Shortening the sentence. Miles is young. If he doesn't have to go away for years, then, well . . ."

"I guess. Actually, Ben, you're making me feel a teeny-tiny little bit less depressed."

"That's what I'm here for."

The windowless room is small, hot, and dusty. There are two metal folding chairs and a metal table. She's been told to wait in here. Where else would she go? Seeing her son is all she can focus on. Josie's phone call wasn't helpful. She needed her sister to tell her there was still hope and to give her at least one reason why. But there is no reason. She knows that. When she broke the news to Richie, he looked bewildered, as if bombings weren't supposed to occur outside the battlefield. He asked if Miles had been hurt, which made her worry he'd forgotten that Miles had fought not in but against the war.

Quince, too, needs to know, he does, but phoning him feels like such a chore. If he says anything derogatory about Miles, she'll . . . But he won't. He loves Miles too. So does Sam. Why else would be stay up all those hours?

What she can't tell anyone about, what she's ashamed to admit to, even to herself, is the surge of relief that spun through her when she heard that Miles was somewhere she could find him. When he was thirteen and hadn't come home by midnight, she sent Johnny out looking for him. And sat in the living room anticipating an accident, a mugging, a stabbing, her son in some emergency room, alone, bleeding. By the time Miles came home, it was close to dawn. She was so relieved to see him she sent him to bed without a promise of punishment. It's how she feels now. If only they let her see, hear, and touch him, she won't complain.

The woman who led her to the room said Miles would be brought by in a few minutes. It's been more than thirty minutes. Where is he? Did they forget she's waiting? His mother? Does that matter?

She opens the door and peers into an empty, dimly lit hallway. If she goes looking for information and isn't here when Miles is brought . . . No, she has to wait, no matter how long, even till dark. She will stay in this room until she sees her son. Dear lord, make it happen soon.

He might need some money. She does have cash with her. But will he be allowed to keep it? Won't they take away all his belongings? Or does that happen after an indictment?

The door opens. She freezes into a statue with a racing heart as a guard ushers in her son. With the table behind her to keep her upright, she determines not to cry. On his first day of school, her tears had so alarmed him he clung to her.

Miles's wrists are cuffed, his ankles as well. He's wearing grimy, worn-at-the-knees pants, an old work shirt, scuffed moccasins, no socks; his hair is dyed auburn. For a split second, she takes him in as he appears, but that dissolves, and it's Miles, her son, boy, teen, man, each aspect as present in his face as in her heart.

He hobbles over to her.

"Baby." She wraps her arms around his lean body, which doesn't resist the pressure of her embrace.

"What's there to say, right?" He tries to smile, but his expression is anxious, intense, his eyes alert, waiting for God knows what.

She touches his cheek; it feels hot. Maybe he has a fever. "We have the best legal team. And your brothers, the family, Josie, we're all here for you every step of the way. Are you reading me?"

He nods. "We'll talk." His voice low, secretive, just between the two of them.

"Yes, we'll spend lots of time together." The guard is tapping his elbow, ready to take him away. Is this all she gets, a few paltry minutes?

"Mom . . . I . . . Yeah, okay." His vulnerability tears at her innards. She can't keep him safe. What kind of mother is she?

"As soon as they allow it, I'll visit, no matter where you are, even in Timbuktu. The family will visit as well. You won't be abandoned."

Once more she wraps her arms around him, wanting to absorb his very substance, reluctant to let him go, the guard eyeing her pensively. "No doubt the food's lousy, but you'll need your strength," she says.

"So will you," he whispers close to her ear.

"Don't be afraid," she whispers back.

The guard takes hold of his elbow, leads him out.

"I love you," she croaks, unsure if he hears.

-34-

She walks slowly through the old Belmont area, not far from the Bronx Zoo. Beneath the El, sunspots dot the street like measles. Small shops edge a square, which includes the bar where she and Celia met the day the bombing of the draft board was announced. Miles has been topic number one in the press. The coverage hasn't been friendly. She prays he doesn't see any of it.

Celia cautioned her to say nothing about Miles's arrest. But who's to say her mother doesn't already know? Johnny would be on it ad nauseam. Didn't he warn Josie that no good would come of all this militancy? Shit. She doesn't want to deal with Johnny, not in her head and not in person. She'll spend an hour there and hope to leave before either Johnny or Terry returns home. She's only here as a favor to Celia, who was supposed to visit their mother and asked her to go instead. She wanted to say no, that she had other . . . but how could she? Celia's exhausted, every day something else about Miles that has to be dealt with.

Entering the old gray brick elevator building, she remembers the first and only time she was here before. It was after Johnny and Terry moved in. Then the rooms were empty of furniture except for a bed and table. Then she was still in school, a freshman, and leaving home to find another way of life was only a fantasy. It's nearly impossible to hold in her head all that has happened since.

Richie once wrote that in Vietnam every day was a lifetime. She can't say that, but her days have been filled with so many experiences it would take a book to list them all.

The apartment is on the sixth floor. She walks through the heavily furnished rooms: motel-type paintings on the walls, doodads stalking one another on multiple shelves, windows covered in drapes that dull the light, and not a book in sight, though glossy magazines are everywhere.

The kitchen is brighter than the other rooms; perhaps it's the overhead light or the Swiss-dotted window curtains. A round wooden table with six chairs centers the room. As soon as she sits, her mother places dish after dish of food in front of her. Cooking for Terry and Johnny, who both work, must keep her mother busy, but feeding her youngest, is that a sign of welcome? It's difficult to know. Her mother finds explanations exhausting, which she learned at a young age. It was her father who answered questions, though with few words to spare.

To her surprise, her mother brings a cup of espresso to the table and joins her.

"I miss Pa," Josie says.

Her mother nods as if to say, Of course.

"You must miss him a lot."

Once more her mother nods but dismissively.

She cuts a thin slice of the thick lasagna, wonders if her mother will ask her anything about her life: how she is doing or what kind of job she has or even if there is anyone special in her life. It's possible these questions about her have been asked of and answered by her siblings.

Her mother pushes the bread basket closer to her. "What about Richie?"

"He's doing okay. Manhattan is easier for him to get around in. My friends visit him, so he has company." She feels the need to defend her choice to remove him from the Bronx.

"Good." Her mother looks thinner, narrower, less robust than she once was.

"Ma? Are you okay living here with Johnny?"

"What else should I do?"

"I guess you could move in with Celia."

"One child or another, it's the same. It's their house, not mine."

"But you can't live alone."

Her mother shrugs.

"You need to say what you want. Otherwise others will make decisions for you."

"Johnny's a good son."

"Of course he is. But none of us know what's in your head."

"What do you mean? I'm not crazy."

"No, no. That's not what I'm say—"

"You don't know anything about what's in my head."

"Tell me."

Her mother pushes the salad platter closer to her.

"Lasagna's delicious, Ma."

"Good."

"So, tell me what's in your head."

"Josie, too many questions come out of your mouth. Always. The world doesn't owe you answers."

"I want to know more about you." Is this true?

Her mother laughs, but it's a harsh sound. "How would your life get better knowing more about mine? What's the point of so much talking? The same in the old country, empty words, not worth the breath it took. No different here. Maybe worse, because everyone wants to hear what they want to hear. I get tired of it."

Her mother's face, still round, is heavily creased, her once-dark hair mostly gray.

"Pa talked about the old country. But you never do."

"What's to talk about?"

"You grew up there. You must—"

"It was bad, poor, wet when it should've been dry, cold when it should've been hot. Complaints, that's all that happened there."

"But you and Pa fell in love."

"Love. Americans think that word is an answer to everything. Not for me. Not for Pa either."

"But you loved each other," she says again, needing it to be so.

Her mother doesn't flinch from her gaze. "Why do you have to know this? What is so important about our lives? We grew up knowing nothing except what we found out for ourselves. All this information everyone here wants, as if it will fill the belly or pay the rent."

She sounds angry, even cheated. Josie hadn't heard that before. She recognized her father's sadness in his nostalgia. But in her mother she only ever saw stoicism. She isn't sure how to respond. Except it's so rare for her mother to offer any insight into herself.

"You sound angry. Are you—"

"Why not?"

"Didn't you and Pa live together happily?"

For a moment her mother looks past her. "Living here was a joke, a joke on us. No matter how hard we worked . . . always the scrimping, nothing to hold on to for tomorrow but worries. Your father wanted lots of children. Not me. It's what he knew. It's how it was in the old country. Have more and more children; each child brings its own luck, people said. But there was no luck there and no luck here. Your father was one of fifteen children. My mother died when I was ten. My father remarried. There are sisters I never knew, because I was already here. It's wrong, how life is handed out. All we could do was to keep on keeping on. Pa was tired. Me too."

Is her mother revealing a truth or disposing of it? "You never talked about your feelings before." Her response hesitant, measured. She's afraid to undercut or disturb this strange moment of sharing, if that's what it is.

Her mother says nothing. The espresso cup empty, at any moment she'll get up and leave the table.

"I wanted to tell Pa about what I've learned about his and my lives. But he died before I could do that. Do you want to know how I spend my time?"

Her mother's eyes open wide, as if she was expecting to be handed bad news.

"Ma. I realize I haven't visited. But I've been involved—"

"I'm not mad at you," her mother suddenly says.

"But I should've made time to—"

"A mother who expects too much from children will be disappointed. You have your own busy lives. I never went back to see my father in the old country. Then he was dead. I was alive and bringing up my children. It's how it goes, all of life, like the hands of a clock, in only one direction." She gets up and begins to clear the table.

Amber light spills across the floor from the three new living room lamps. The faux-leather club chair is new too, but the low marble coffee table is one that she and Melvin brought home from the Salvation Army. Instead of posters, a Navajo blanket she found at a street fair covers a large patch of wall. Open to a May breeze, two long windows await blinds that still must be bought.

The TV drones the eleven o'clock news. She and Richie are on the couch watching, but he rarely comments on whatever's going on. During the Pentagon action planning meetings at the apartment, he listens to the jabber but won't give up his thoughts. Perhaps unearthing even a sentence would loose an avalanche.

Over the last several weeks, she's gotten used to his silences; still, she's grateful for his presence. Their shared past leaves her less lonely. She told him about the visit to their mother, that she entered the apartment a child and left feeling more like an adult. How crazy was that? But he understood, said that Ma had the ability to both confuse and provoke. He is her brother after all.

The phone rings. Calls this late are never good—her mother's words. She reaches over to lift the receiver.

"Hello."

"We just got word"—it's Celia's anxious whisper—"about a

date for Miles's trial. It's soon, sooner than expected. He's glad about it. Told me nothing could be worse than Rikers. I'm not prepared for a verdict. I want to keep hold of my hopes."

"I understand. It's nerve-racking. Is Sam asleep?"

"Think so. Am I whispering?"

"Are you okay? I mean, I know you can't be totally okay, but—"

"Josie, I can't sleep. Nightmares wake me, but the daytime feels just as bad. I keep trying to hear Paul in my head. He'd be giving me one reassuring sentence after another. But I can't hear him anymore. My head's too filled with fearsome thoughts. Miles keeps telling me that he's fine, that he'll get through it. But he's pale with fright. He's my son. I know him. He can't fool me. And—"

"Let's meet for a drink after work. I'll come up to the Bronx."

She's never heard her sister sound so defeated.

"Can't. I'm meeting with the attorney. He told me to bring Sam, wants to prep him in case he's called as a character witness. Sam would be a terrible witness. He's furious about what Miles has done to our family; at least that's how he puts it. I don't want Sam on the stand. I'm—"

"Celia, Sam won't be called," she says with certainty, though how would she know? But she needs to bring down her sister's distress.

"Is Richie still awake?"

"Want to talk to him?"

"Not now. Say hi to him."

"Okay. Have some wine."

"I already am."

She replaces the receiver. "Celia says hi."

Thing is, she's not ready for the trial either. It's the cap on the bottle, the lock on the door. Miles sent to God knows where for God knows how long if not forever. Most of his visiting time is spent with Celia or an attorney. She saw him once. He didn't say much, his face drawn, his hair buzz cut, the auburn gone, no more glasses, just the dark, fiery eyes. She tried to be upbeat, but he's as aware as she is of what's coming. She, Ben, and a few others are working to raise funds for his defense, but the response has been less than generous. The wealthy liberals who gave money to other funds do not find the actions of Miles's collective defensible. At work, too, there are nasty comments from colleagues who don't know Miles is her nephew. Ben cautions her not to respond, that it would only endanger her job, and how would that help Miles? He has a point.

She won't share these thoughts with Richie, won't be the one to add anxiety to his daily dose of discomfort. The least she can do is to protect him from her fears.

Suddenly, there on the TV screen is Melvin in jeans and a T-shirt, his big eyes blazing, finger pointing, as he harangues Black students at some southern university to get more involved. Her riveted focus feasts on Melvin's face, her breathing caught somewhere too deep to access. Then the twenty-second blip is over.

"Do you want another beer? I'm going to have one," she says.
"Always welcome."

When she turns on the kitchen light, the brightness feels like an affront. She extracts two beers from the fridge and returns to the living room, where the screen is now on a commercial. She takes a long swallow, and the cold bitterness reaches into the pit of her stomach as car headlights shoot past the windows like bullets.

With Richie in bed, she tries to focus on the TV screen, but Melvin has climbed back into her head, where it hurts to have him. How dare he take up vital space? A twenty-second TV blip, that's all it was, a finger pointing . . . the words lost on her. She ought to visit a shrink or a shaman, someone, anyone, that can erase the hurt and sense of loss that shadows her. She remembers how in that dark Broadway bar Melvin shivered in a leather jacket that couldn't keep him warm. Yet there he was on TV in only a T-shirt and jeans, doing his thing without a thought about her. And here she is, allowing him back into her thoughts, where he no longer resides every day. Hasn't enough time passed for her to be able to take in the good work he's doing without feeling haunted? No answer.

A loud, frenzied, hoarse noise comes from Richie's bedroom. She's heard him struggle through many nightmares. Tonight, though, it sounds as if something has him by the throat.

She switches on his bedside lamp, opening a pool of light. His eyes are shut tight. His head moves from side to side as if trying to rid itself of whatever chases him. The frightening sound continues to gurgle out from deep in his throat.

"Richie. Wake up. It's me, Josie." She clasps one of his shoulders and shakes him. Maybe waking him is wrong. Maybe only in nightmares can he work out the demons that plague him. Yet she can't leave him in such anguish. She calls his name, louder, again and again, and then places her hand lightly on his forehead to still his head. His eyes open.

"Richie. It's me, Josie. You're having a nightmare."

He lies very still; his eyes steady on her.
"Are you okay?"
He nods.
She waits a few minutes, not sure if he's truly awake.
"Go to bed," he mumbles and sounds exhausted.
"I could stay . . ."
"No . . . Don't turn the lamp off."
This fucking war, she thinks, leaving his door ajar.

-36-

Josie sits on the edge of the bed. The room is hot, humid. Dark clouds gather beneath a mackerel sky. She prays the threatening weather isn't an omen. She has to get dressed. But a fearsome inertia refuses to let go. If she moves, the day will begin. It will continue. It will reveal all that she will never be ready to know.

Her memory has opened the vault on scenes she has no wish to remember. Miles slipping on ice, screaming in pain, his arm broken, while she stood there, helpless, holding the cord on the sled they never got to use. The childish pact they made to live together that unraveled because they couldn't agree on where that would be. Miles chose California. She insisted on Mexico. Why? Who knows, except it was even farther away than California. Would Miles remember any of this, or has the present nightmare sent the past too far back for him to retrieve? Miraculously, he manages to get through each court session without looking entirely depressed. Perhaps it's being together with his friends at the defendants' table, while in jail they've been kept separate.

She's on a brief leave of absence from work, and she and Richie have shown up in the courtroom every day. With his full beard and long shaggy hair, wearing a T-shirt, jeans, and sandals, he's quite a sight sitting in the front row. Celia, too, is there every day. Today, however, everyone will be present.

Slipping into a blouse and skirt, she heads for the kitchen to make coffee and places three mugs on the table. Ben will arrive in a few minutes to drive them down. Now that he's working nights at the movement printing press, he shows up every day to help out, for which she's grateful and relieved. Richie on public transportation isn't easy to watch. It takes him forever to maneuver the subway steps. Cane, step down, right foot, left foot—she can almost hear it repeating in his head like a mantra.

Pouring coffee into the mugs, she replays once more the past weeks of testimony, some of which was surprising, none more so than that given by the informer who infiltrated Miles's collective. A man in his late twenties, clean shaven with short reddish hair, who spoke softly and favorably about the collective, said how concerned they were not to hurt anyone, how they once put off the action because a wino lingered in a nearby alcove, how they consistently talked about the frustration of not being able to stop the war despite the increasing number of people taking to the streets to protest.

Although last week the jury came back with a guilty verdict, she fervently hopes the judge will consider the informer's words in his sentencing today. These are extraordinary times. People are being defined by their stance on the war.

The low thud of Richie's cane approaches the kitchen. He's in his military dress uniform, Purple Heart pinned to the breast pocket, his beard shaved off and his hair pulled into a ponytail. He says nothing and sits to drink his coffee. A shiver of fear runs through her. Has he lost it? Has the trial and all the talk about the war sent him back there in his head? She wants to know but doesn't ask, too afraid of the answers.

The high-domed courtroom ceiling gives the place a church-like look, but there's nothing spiritual here. Only the occasional wail of police sirens interrupts the drone of voices. People fill every bench. It's been this way most days; newspaper articles about the case appear daily. A number of reporters lean on pea-green walls while much of the rest of the press lingers outside the double doors.

Richie's uniform causes a family buzz. She expects even the judge will notice. Johnny, too, is in uniform. Terry has her arm around Sam, who doesn't look pleased. Quince has come down for the sentencing. Only her mother has been spared the ordeal. She sits between Celia and her cousin Grace, who relented and called her family a few weeks ago.

Miles in a dark suit, the jacket drooping past his narrow shoulders, is brought in with his three young codefendants, also wearing suits. Along with their attorneys, they sit at a long table covered with folders and yellow pads. With a puzzled look, Miles takes in Richie's military uniform.

Carrying her paraphernalia, the stenographer hurries in ahead of the judge.

"All rise for His Honor."

Voices lower as the judge takes a seat. Grace links her arm with Josie's. Josie takes Celia's hand. The judge, in his sixties, is short, tired looking, with dark hooded eyes and skin that seems to hang off a once-round face. He has the high-pitched voice of an auctioneer. She'd avoid him at a party, but now her eyes are trained on him.

No doubt the judge has spent hours considering the words he's about to deliver, but she wants only to know how many years Miles will have to serve. The judge begins his presentation without prelude.

"Society is made up of laws . . . even if the motive . . . Young men, still . . . And it is a turbulent time . . ."

When she was little and lost her beloved heart-shaped locket, she was inconsolable. Her father wanted to know why she was sobbing. After she told him why, he smacked her arm in disgust, said that only the loss of another should cause such misery. Anything else could be replaced. She wonders now if his words included the loss of years.

". . . sentenced to not less than twenty and . . . to be served . . . So be it." The judge bangs his gavel to mark the close of his decision.

Richie, who can't exercise much agility, stands and taps a slow path toward the defendants' table a few feet away. The judge orders him to sit down. He continues to walk. The judge begins to bang his gavel.

With one hand on his cane, Richie leans over and pins his Purple Heart medal on Miles's jacket. Everyone is stunned, Miles most of all.

People stand to see; some move into the aisle to get a better look at her brother. A cacophony of voices rise, words difficult to make out. There's a smattering of applause.

The judge, himself now half-standing, his face scrunched into exasperation, continues to bang his gavel hard for order.

Richie attempts to return to his seat, but security guards stop him. Johnny, fleet on his feet, arrives at Richie's side and says something to the head security honcho. Who knows what cops say to one another?

With his hand on Richie's shoulder, Johnny steers him toward the exit, but another guard blocks their path and grabs Richie's arm. The cane clatters to the floor.

A howl of protest wells up inside her. She stands ready to go help Richie.

Celia pulls her back. "Let it play out. Don't make it worse."

Up at the bench, the attorneys now spin words only the judge can hear. Johnny, Richie, the guard, remain frozen in place, a still life of before the after. All wait for the next moments.

The judge must have pity, be exhausted, or fear tomorrow's headline—Wounded War Hero Wrestled to the Ground—because he lets her brother off with a reprimand.

Johnny picks up the cane and returns it to Richie. People step aside to make room as Richie slowly taps his way up the aisle, a glint of satisfaction in his smile. And she gets it: everything must be earned, even redemption.

As Artie promised, the restaurant has sawdust on the floor and ancient waiters. It's seems clear that ordering anything other than a steak would be blasphemous. Though he asked her out months ago, life intruded, and she never took him up on it. Then seeing him at Miles's trial, she was moved and arranged to have dinner with him.

"Thank you for coming to the trial."

"No big deal. How are you doing?"

"It depends."

"On what?" Artie's straightforwardness takes getting used to.

"In one way, I'm glad the trial is over, but in another I wish it wasn't. I think about Miles all the time, worry about how he's being treated. I work myself into a state of anxiety that only abates when I visit." Has she said too much? "Does that make any sense?"

"Celia, you don't know how not to make sense."

"I don't think that's true, but thank you."

"How is your brother Richie?"

"What do you mean?"

"After that stunt at the trial, I wondered if there were repercussions."

"No. But my sister says he's back in his virtual cave." A stab of guilt assails her. She hasn't called or visited Richie since the trial ended a while ago. Busy with her new job and traveling to visit Miles, and then there's Sam and—

"Another drink?" Artie asks.

"I've already had two."

He shrugs his big shoulders as if to say, What does that matter?

They're driving along the bumpy dirt road leading away from the prison. Artie's a slow, careful driver. The only radio station without static offers country music. In the past weeks, he's been kind, showing up at her place with food and wine, phoning her often. Sam doesn't seem to mind Artie's visits. Or if he does, he's chosen to share his angst with Maria, not her. So far, Sam hasn't wanted to visit Miles, and she hasn't pushed him.

Attica, Miles told her, was the name of an ancient Greek territory, which made them both laugh because the visitors' room, with its chicken wire fence and bolted-to-the-floor tables, defies even a semblance of civilization. In some ridiculous and ludicrous way, she's adjusted to speaking to him in a place as uninviting as this one is. It amazes her how much a being can adapt to. And she continues to hope that the slow seep of acceptance is also happening for Miles. He doesn't complain or won't to her.

At first she feared finding him depressed, distraught, or worse. But he was soon part of a group that was organizing prisoners to make common demands about horrible conditions. Miles assured her it wasn't about expecting the comforts of home, just the right to exist as human beings.

She hasn't missed a visit since he's been there, but her brief time with Miles is never enough. They talk about his father, her father, everyone in between. They discuss politics, government, religion, philosophy, class, or he does. He's proud of his background, says that working-class people are like blue jays, ubiquitous but beautiful when they fly. He's become her teacher. She's become the repository of his thoughts. He told her how the collective came to its decisions, how most of the time he was afraid. He said he was sorry to be caught but not sorry about saving the lives of potential draftees. Did doubt cross her face? "Mom," he said, "change is like the wind. Can you see the wind?" She's grateful that he isn't filled with regret, a useless, painful emotion.

"Did it go well?" Artie interrupts her thoughts to ask the same question he asks after each visit. She's thankful that he drives her and that he waits outside the prison until she's done. It's not his son.

"Okay, I suppose." And hears the desultory tone of her own voice. "Each departure feels like a rending."

His large hand slides over to squeeze hers.

The car rumbles past untamed brush, weedy fields, and embedded boulders with no house in sight, a landscape more strange than beautiful. Birds flit from one side of the road to the other; their songs enter the open windows. With Miles locked away from nature, she believes it's her duty to see everything.

A man's figure lopes into the center of the road from nowhere it seems, and Artie stops the car.

He's tall, skinny, wearing a faded blue baseball cap and short-sleeve shirt tucked into jeans, his feet in sandals. He looks old, his cheeks sunken, but there's no gray in the reddish-brown hair leaking out of the cap.

With hand edge to brow, the man salutes them.

"What's up?" Artie asks in his usual gruff voice.

"I'd appreciate a lift to the highway. You can say no or yes."

Artie looks at her. She shrugs, though he could have a gun in his pocket. But he looks fragile, and he's already climbing into the back seat.

"Call me Paco, not the name I was born with. Then again, I don't know who that was." He rests his chin on the front seat between them, releasing a piney scent. "Coming from the prison," the man states.

She nods.

"A brother?"

"My son."

"Terrible place but no worse than some outdoor areas I know."

"That's one way to look at it," Artie mutters.

"When you accurately describe a situation, you own it," the man says with a certainty that surprises her. "On the other hand, if you can't see it straight, you're lost." He looks at her. "Your son . . . what's he in for?"

"He's a political prisoner," she says surprising herself and no doubt Artie as well.

"Political prisoners disagree with the system, and those who agree own the jail keys," the man says "When the situation reverses, the other side gets the keys."

"He fought against the Vietnam War," she tells him, not sure why.

"War does it every time. Don't matter which one. Whoever makes it home is a survivor. No house big enough to store his baggage."

Having him gaze at her is disconcerting.

"There are two ways to survive," the man continues. "A person can be filled with hate or with love; either one provides energy to keep life going."

He drops each word as if it's an omen.

"The present war is an immoral undertaking. On the other hand, it will teach us not to engage this way again. So it's unworthy and worthy."

Is he putting them on? Maybe he's one of those itinerant preachers. Or maybe her need for solace knows no boundaries.

"Have you taken note of the strange doings?" he suddenly asks in a lowered voice. "Earrings on men, wild hair on everyone, long dresses in the morning?"

"There are reasons for not conforming," Miles told her. Being out of order upsets the expectable, forces people to really see, not just look, he said. But she has no desire to share this with Paco.

"So you live in those fields," Artie says.

"My body resides there and at times elsewhere."

"Where will you go after we drop you off?" she asks.

"I don't know. But I do know the state troopers around here aren't friendly."

"I guess we've been lucky," Artie mumbles.

"No such thing as luck," the man states. He starts to cough, deep, rasping, phlegm-filled exertions, and closes his eyes. "Rest your eyes and your body rests," he says more to himself and leans back in the seat taking his piney scent with him.

"Paco," she calls softly, "are you okay?"

"Either you heal or you die," he murmurs.

They're approaching the ramp that leads to the highway. Maybe they should take him to a hospital or—

"I'll get out here." His hand on the door handle.

"But it's nowhere; I mean, you won't get another—"

"I'll manage or I won't." He climbs out slowly, then stands to the side and once more salutes them.

"Odd bugger," Artie says, as the car speeds toward the highway. "At first it seemed he saw everything in black or white, but actually he's stuck in the gray zone."

She glances at Artie's large face with hardly a definition of bone, and a tinge of admiration spirals into consciousness. She hadn't seen him as thoughtful before, and like a new view of an old picture, it surprises and comforts her.

-38-

Except for Ben, who sits beside her, the last of Josie's friends have left. Her mother hasn't moved from Celia's overstuffed club chair, her eyes two dry wells. Grace kneads her aunt's hands as if healing were possible. Quince and Sam are sprawled on the floor; neither one has said more than a few words all night. Johnny and Terry huddle together on the couch. Richie sits near the window. Artie is in the kitchen making yet another pot of coffee, though it's almost midnight. A blanket of sorrow smothers banalities, and pain radiates from every corner of the room. There's no comfort to give and none to take either.

Ben has adopted her family because his own is made up of "just parents." But danger lurks in large families; disaster can fell members one by one. She told him as much last night when he drove her home to pick up fresh clothing. While she packed a small bag, he lay on the bed, his eyes steady on her, his curly hair splayed on the pillow, his T-shirt pulled tight across his chest, and the emptiness inside her became unbearable. Without a word she fit in beside him. Like some underwater creature, he folded himself around her, his scent more familiar than expected, his arms stronger than anticipated, his body inviting, and the rest more natural than she could've hoped for.

-39-

Celia wipes the last of the hair from the bathroom sink and flushes away the tissues. She gazes in the mirror at the delicate veins crisscrossing the tight cap of her scalp. The baldness gives her a bold appearance that will change with time, though the absence of Miles will be constant.

During their last visit, Miles told her nothing could compete with his sense of well-being when fighting for justice. She'll hold on to that. But it won't be enough. It won't provide the warm flesh she craves to touch, the burning eyes that refresh her soul. It won't give her a chance to one day share a movie or coffee with him, to see him approach or leave, to hear his soft singing. He won't surprise, upset, or please her ever again. How will she endure that? She contains his past, some of his recent present, but the elimination of his future is where the agony resides.

When the prison authorities finally let her see him, he was laid out on a gurney, a sheet covering his body but not his face, the cast of his expression caught in midthought, so much left unsaid. She would've stood there for hours, but someone told her she had to leave and ushered her out.

After the funeral, with arms around her, loving voices talked to her nonstop. But what is it she's supposed to accept—the hole at the core of her being, the weight of all the leftover love? She doesn't want closure; the pain will keep him with her.

She unlocks the bathroom door. It creaks as it always has. She's lived here for many years. The house contains walls, ceilings, and floors made into home only by its inhabitants; Miles took a piece of it with him.

Barefoot, she pads into the living room. Richie glances at her without surprise. Her sons stare at her. Her mother gasps and Johnny looks disappointed. Josie, who's said little these past days, watches her as if Celia has become a fragile thing.

Touching her bald head, she says, "I did this for Miles. I will never again conform," then kneels beside her sons. "Whatever you felt about his politics, Miles knew how much you both loved him." Then pressing Quince's arm, she says, "If the Point orders you to Vietnam, you can't go. I lost one son to the war, and I will not lose another. Do you understand?" Her voice strong and certain.

His eyes wide, Quince nods. Maybe Quince believes that in time she'll mellow. She won't. Or in the end he'll disobey her. She can't know that now. But she'll fight his going there with all of her strength and, if necessary, sit in at his commander's office until the orders are rescinded.

-40-

In bed beside her sister, Josie wakes from another fitful night. The relentless rain against the windows brings the raw, wet earth of the burial site into the room. The loneliness of Miles, left to the elements, loneliness that chills her bones.

With all the wailing, weeping people at the funeral, their mouths contorted in pain, there seemed no room for her anguish. Tears fell from her eyes, yes, but it wasn't Miles she was viewing; it was a body in a coffin, his spirit his essence gone, and it frightened her. When her father died, for days, maybe weeks, after, she'd have to remind herself that he was dead. A sense of numbness filled her then. Not so now. Miles enters her mind as soon as her eyes open, and she wants to reach out to him.

Quince and Sam asleep in the next room have quietly taken over food shopping and cooking, though no one is particularly hungry. Guests still arrive and sit for a while but only in the kitchen. The rest of the house holds a silence so complete it seems as if each room has been sealed off in Saran Wrap.

She watches Celia manage the empty hours of the day with an emotional strength that can only be assigned to her role as mother. Though during the night when Celia weeps quietly, she's there to encircle her shoulders. Unable to abandon her sister, she will stay a while longer. More than a generous impulse, it's also out of a hope that remaining here will somehow lessen her misery.

The small bedside clock tells her it's nearly dawn; she's made it through another long night.

Heading to the Bronx Zoo, Josie walks past the shuttered houses, the bike-strewn lawns, and a few sad-looking trees. The dimming streetlights emit a foggy orange glow, the damp air cool, somewhere the faint rumble of a garbage truck digesting. The sky is cloudy, the gray-pebbled sidewalks cracked and uneven. Soon the early morning rush to work will fill the empty streets with cars and buses.

Only a week ago she and Ben stood outside Attica waiting, hoping for a positive solution. Though it was September, a nasty wind blew, and rain turned the rutted lane muddy. More and more people collected outside to support the striking prisoners. While she envisioned Miles huddled with the strikers, others saw him on TV within the semicircle of those who were negotiating demands. Demands so reasonable she thought it had to be settled peaceably. After two days the rain stopped; the crowd grew. She and Ben inched closer and closer to the prison. Then on the fifth day, as the first flecks of light appeared in the predawn sky, the air exploded with the noise of helicopters. Lines of uniformed men ran shouting toward the prison yard. The sounds of gunshots and hideous shrieks went through her like electric currents. Her legs gave way, and she slid to the ground. Ben knelt beside her, tears streaming down his face.

The last time they spoke Miles had explained the upcoming strike, the growing relationship between white and Black prisoners, and how much he was learning, his voice soft yet insistent. Thinner than ever, growing a beard, his eyes rapt with concentration. Inmates in the visiting room had stopped to whisper in his ear, drop a handshake, slap his back; he was one among a community of men in sync with one another. No doubt he remains in many hearts. There's relief in not being the only one carrying him.

Reaching the park, she climbs the hidden alley-slim path into the main road of the zoo. Once inside, she feels disconnected from all who know her, a sense of aloneness as visceral as the slick black macadam beneath her feet.

The surrounding bushes surrender rainwater as she pushes past to climb the stones. At the flat top of the rock, the usual vista appears and for a split second so too the old memory of anonymity.

She sits on the edge of the rock, legs dangling, the ghost of him beside her. "Miles," she whispers, "was the bombing worth it? Dying so young, what good can come of that?" She can almost hear him say it's the wrong question. But he risked his life so easily. Didn't he think about those left behind? Didn't they matter? Surely he couldn't have known he'd be caught; surely he couldn't have known he'd die. So why blame him for the outcome? Though something in her does. He was her confidant, an alter ego, the one who absorbed all she was learning. When he refused to share his secrets, she felt betrayed, not protected. But with him it was always about results being loftier than process. Mao said a daily teaspoon of earth removed from the mountain would reduce it in time or something to that effect. But that was too slow for Miles, who needed change then and there. She shares his impatience, doesn't she? His death a lesson she still has to learn.

Taking a last look at the swath of park below, the shimmering wet leaves, the distant houses, each with its own story, she can't imagine coming here again and wonders how many endings occur in a lifetime.

-41-

The late-October air has turned cold. Wind moves the rosy-cheeked treetops. Her eyes feast on the crowded DC streets. The first time she was here for a demonstration, Melvin led her through the inner city to give her a tour she didn't know she would be getting. Now she's able to find her way without help. The war, however, still rages on.

At first when Celia told her it was time for her to go back home, she felt rebuffed. Thought her sister no longer wanted to commiserate with her about Miles. They both loved him, didn't they? It was Richie who said that Celia's loss is different than hers. Of course it is. Each death is personal; so, too, the grief.

The area in front of the Capitol Building is cordoned off. She can hear the applause, whistles, and rallying cries as the Vietnam veterans begin to form a line. Even the few who may have arrived to heckle seem chastened by what they see: men with ravaged expressions who are trying to redeem something they can't define. They include the walking wounded, those in wheelchairs, in military dress uniform, in grunt gear, in civvies, and there's no end in sight to the line. It's a public venting, and the veterans, together as one, are claiming the day.

The line snakes past a huge metal trash can. One after another the veterans toss their medals inside; some are flipped across the rim, others placed in gently, like babes into a crib. She hones in on one young face, bearded, red bandana circling the veteran's forehead, big Afro grazing his shoulders, tattoos climbing his arms. His torso naked beneath a leather vest—weather be damned. He wants to say a few words at the nearby mic . . . He tries . . . It's not happening, emotion clogging his throat. Another veteran rushes up to bear him away. Their collective grief, sorrow, revulsion, are housed inside her.

Richie should be here, truly he should. He's one of them. But when she asked him to go, he said, "Too much." Now watching the veteran's faces, she understands what Richie meant. Still, it would've been good for him to be with other veterans. He's alone a lot of the time, and even when she's at home, he's so quiet. It's as if his life has passed and he's living off only memories, and how good can they be? He's agreed to continue physical therapy and even maybe—he's not sure—take a course somewhere. But the brother she grew up with, she can't find him anywhere.

Finally, the line of veterans is getting shorter. Still, she's reluctant to leave, but she must. Tomorrow, women from across the nation will gather in force to march to the Pentagon and camp out there overnight. There's still much to do for the event. She hadn't planned to become so involved, but the best laid plans . . . At the rally, she will give the opening speech.

The makeshift office is in the dank, cold basement of an Episcopal church. Volunteers remain busy with last-minute details. Tall-lettered slogans written on large white cardboard sheets lean against the walls. A few side-by-side milk crates serve as desks. Three temporary phones have been installed so they can answer the constant calls. Definitely a good sign, they all agree. Maisie, Nina, and others are out on DC streets leafleting people with the details about tomorrow's march.

Though there's chatter, busyness is all. Paying scant attention to anything being said around her, she takes a seat behind one of the makeshift desks. When the phone rings, she answers: "Hello this is the planning site for—"

"I need to talk to Josie Russo."

It's no voice she recognizes.

"I don't have all day," he warns.

"Who is this?"

"Give her a message." His voice gruff.

"Who is this?"

"Melvin Curtis was shot dead doing what he never should've been doing on a southern campus." He hangs up, but she continues to hold the receiver until an operator's loud, robot-like voice informs her that the phone is off—

Replacing the receiver, she looks around to see that no one has noticed her distress, though she's finding it difficult to breathe.

Getting up to lean against a wall beneath the porthole-shaped window, her skin straitjacket tight, she's still having difficulty breathing. Her fingers are icy, her limbs heavy, her brain numb. She watches several women continue to answer the phones. Nearby laughter sounds distorted, a record on the wrong speed. Once, when she was eight, a boy was shot near where she was standing. She froze. Someone had to carry her home. She thinks to slide down the wall to find ground, but nothing will help. The man's words stunned her like a middle-of-the-night obscene call. Staring into empty space, she can neither see nor focus. But isn't this exactly what provocateurs do to muck up demonstrations? She knows that, doesn't she? The call could be just that, meant to disrupt, perhaps even to keep her from delivering her speech at the rally. Didn't Melvin tell her how the Panthers received hundreds of impossible messages, then went on to do whatever was necessary? She will too. Melvin would expect no less.

Careful to avoid a glimpse of anyone's grief, concerned that someone might recognize her, she slips into a back pew, on guard against any who might open the wound.

Loud piano chords startle the room into silence. Someone begins to play and sing the Nina Simone's song "Mississippi Goddam" as men and women in Panther uniform march in through two side doors to stand guard at the mahogany casket, but who can harm him now? Her eyes go to the first pew, where his mother sits. The church doors remain open. There are more people than seats, and many will listen to the service from outside. It's North Carolina, and the winds are friendly.

Voices have been hushed, but the air vibrates with tension. Or maybe it's the haunting music with its contrary lyrics that wring the heart. Because whoever killed Melvin is still eating, sleeping, making love. Some cop, sheriff, or who knows, no one is sure yet, sees a Black man running not away but toward him. Maybe he panics, maybe it's what he's been waiting to do, or maybe he's following orders. Whatever the reason, he shoots. It's unconscionable, unforgivable, sentiments shared by all present. But in truth Josie wishes she hadn't come. Her racing mind churns out unexpected emotions that she doesn't want to feel; it makes her restless, claustrophobic. Even worse, a fist of remembered misery or present grief or surely both presses her chest with such ferocity she isn't sure how to survive it. But if she gets up to leave, attention will focus on her.

It isn't the right time for white and Black to bed down together is what Melvin told her that night. Yet they did bed down together, she and Melvin. Those years happened. Afraid of being thought an impediment to the struggle, she kept the aftermath of resentment to herself. Now Melvin's gone; she's left with their past. What does she do with it?

The minister, in a voluminous maroon robe with sleeves so wide each could fit a child inside, leans over the casket to intone a few words no one can hear. With Bible in hand, he strides up to the pulpit. He's tall and thin, his wispy goatee slightly darker than his brown skin. His eyes slide over faces, and in a voice shaking with contained fury, he proclaims that Melvin should be alive. "He is needed here among us. And it is hard, too hard, to know what use the energy of this man could be put to in heaven. I understand . . . I share . . . your head-shaking wonder at how such a tragedy can have any good in it . . . But he's gone to a better place . . ." And now the words become too familiar to take in anew.

It seems others react the same way. There's a decided stir, clothes rustle, legs shift, feet slide, and then shouts erupt— "Lord, enough is enough!" "Fight back!" "No more!" "Wrong is wrong!" "Justice, Jesus, justice!"—the congregation threatening to become a crowd. And the minister, his hands gripping the sides of the pulpit, studies the scene for so long that she can't help but wonder what he's seeing. But he doesn't ask for calm. No, he isn't talking at all. Instead he steps back, raises his arms signaling them to speak.

And they do, one after the other with not a second between, men, women, young and old. Some speak from the pew, some from the aisle. Some go to the pulpit; still others stand with palm on casket as if it's their heart. And she's listening now, she really is, because they're attempting to resurrect him. Melvin in the fields, factories, voting booths. Melvin visiting the mayor, governor, police chief. Melvin escorting seniors to their benefits, rousing students on campuses, stimulating camaraderie in jail. Melvin organizing strikes, antiwar marches, sit-ins. Melvin teaching kids, speechifying in town centers, preaching in this or that church. Everyone now vowing to continue the fight, promising to carry his message forward. Hope must be taken for granted like water from a tap.

The voices are angry, tearful, and strangely joyous. They're claiming him as their own, taking him in then and there, declaring his consequence to families, communities, and the world at large. More than an outburst, it's an expression of love made palpable. He means so much to so many. It's unforgettable, uplifting. Only his mother remains quiet, because what can she say? Her boy is dead. Still it must count for something, people here from everywhere unwilling to bury him, refusing to let him go, insisting on carrying him with them as they continue the struggle.

And their words are revelatory; they burn into her brain, bring tears to her eyes. Her past with Melvin now redefined as a sudden gift. Laughter, fear, politics, kisses, hopes, and love, she and Melvin shared it all, didn't they? And she's grateful and proud of their years together, a connection as intact as her memories.

The late afternoon sun streams into the church igniting all it touches as the minister closes his Bible. Men line up to lift the casket onto their shoulders. Though it's not what she planned, she'll follow the congregation to the graveside. The minister will read the requisite prayers, and maybe silently she'll recite one of her own.

She removes her sunglasses, slides them into her purse, and prepares to say a few words to Melvin's mother. How could she not?

It's a half mile to the bus stop. The sky is a patchwork of clouds. Ancient trees, wide armed and leafless, promise summer shade; a swing dangles hopefully from a crisscross of branches. Scraggly fields yellow and dry as far as the eye can see. Crisp underbrush tracks the roadside, and sprinklings of tiny blue wild flowers defy the season.

Although she hears dogs barking, none appear. A few houses lean back from the edge of the road as if pushed by an angry hand. She waves to people on a porch, but they simply watch her. What a sight she must be, a white woman in an army jacket over a long green dress.

The Greyhound station is in front of a small general store that sells cigarettes, candy, newspapers, aspirin, shampoo, and toothpaste. That's one side of the shop. On the other are racks of men's shirts and boxes of hiking boots. An old, splintery wooden bench acts as the divider; an even more weathered relic sits outside the store.

Walking up and down aisles, she fingers shot glasses, beer mugs, coffee cups, some dusty and soiled, but no matter. They're not what the store thrives on. The shelves against the wall are filled with bottles of whiskey and wine, a harbinger of winter's early nights cabined with loved ones. Already the ashy twilight darkens the stained floorboards. She collects a newspaper, gum, a cellophane-wrapped honey ham sandwich, and an apron for Ben that reads, *Best cook in town.*

At home, Ben has taken charge of Thanksgiving. He's bought a huge turkey, yams, marshmallows, and apple, pecan, and pumpkin pies. It isn't her thing, though, all that domesticity in one small abode, which happens to be hers and Richie's. But Ben is reassuring, even encouraging. Just watch him whip it all together with only a few inevitable tokes along the way. Family dinner is what he wants.

And everyone has agreed to come, Ben's parents, her mother, Johnny, Terry, Grace, Carla, Celia, Artie, Sam, Quince, and Richie of course. They will eat and drink, and though it's still too difficult, too soon to be merry, they'll be together, which is a start, isn't it?

Placing her wares on the worn countertop, she smiles at the man behind the register, his face and hair as gray brown as the falling night.

"Good evening," she says.

He nods. Begins ringing up each purchase.

"Is the bus usually on time?"

"Oh yes, it is." And for the beat of a second, he waits for her to tell him what he's too polite to ask.

"I'm returning to New York. I was here for Melvin Curtis's funeral."

He plucks a paper bag from some hole beneath the counter. "My grandsons were there."

"Did you know him?"

"Well enough." And he shakes his head sadly. "Have yourself a decent trip now." He hands her the bag.

No surprise that the man behind the counter knew Melvin. Her family has to know about Melvin too. She wants them to take him in for what he meant to her and to so many others. That may take time. Some things are too big to absorb quickly.

Sitting out on the rickety bench in the blue-tinged air filled with the prattle of insects, she detects the scent of burnt coffee, or maybe it's the chicory Melvin talked about. She would've liked to tell Melvin about the hospital's offer to train her as a midwife. Courses at night, job during the day, there'll be scant time for political work. Still, the idea is not without attraction. Eventually she could help open birthing centers in poor neighborhoods. Melvin would like that; he'd want her to continue to make a difference.

As the bus nears, its lights blaze against the falling darkness. But the road ahead is still visible.

ACKNOWLEDGMENTS

A special note of profound gratitude to Dan Simon, publisher, Seven Stories Press, for his belief in my work, and for his integrity, thought, and care that have always been available to me. Thank you. Thank you.

Deep appreciation to my first readers who gave generously of their time and support: Jan Clausen, whose detailed and insightful attention to every nuance made a huge difference, thank you; Jane Lazarre, my talented and constant friend whose knowledge and whose devotion to my work never failed to spur me on. Thank you, Farah Jasmine Griffin, for your astute critiques that opened my thought and made the book more real. Thank you, Liz Gewirtzman, for taking the time to talk through the novel and for offering me the benefit of your insights. Thank you, Wesley Brown, for giving freely of your time to benefit my work and of course for your friendship. Thank you, Tom Engelhardt, for the constant support and ongoing belief in my work, and for always being there. Thank you as well to TomDispatch.com for publishing and disseminating my essays and supporting my books.

With deep appreciation for the friendship and ever-caring support of my work and much more, my profound gratitude to Elizabeth Strout, whose advice is always spot-on.

Thank you, Lauren Hooker, senior editor, Seven Stories Press, for the thoughtful and close care and nurturing of the book, especially during this trying pandemic year. Thank you, Katie Herman, for the insightful copyediting that helped to smooth the wrinkles. Thank you, Nicki Kattoura, Seven Stories Press, for reaching out and for the close reading of my book.

Thank you, Ruth Weiner, director of publicity, Seven Stories Press; I'm forever grateful for your careful attention to my books, past and present, which has made all the difference.

To the entire Seven Stories Staff, my admiration and deep appreciation for your amazing work to usher into the light a beautifully designed book and cover.

And, as always, a zillion thanks to my wonderful agent, Melanie Jackson, a national treasure.

For urging me on and being there when needed, thank you, Vicki Brietbart, Prue Glass, Barbara Schneider, Rina Kleege, Ellen Siegel, Joanne Nagano, Pat Walters, and Marsha Taubenhaus.

And to those who have aided and abetted in ways too numerous to describe, I thank: Denise Campono, Urszula Kopciuch, Cindy Harford, Anika Dobson, and Peggy Belenoff

To my family for their never-ending love and support, I am grateful to Robert and Sam Trestman, Judi Gologorsky Brand, Sam and Yudi Wiggins, and to Dr. Kenneth Trestman for his help and brilliant counsel.

And to the memory of the late Charlie Wiggins, I am ever thankful for his unfailing belief in the writing of this book.

I remain now and always profoundly grateful to Georgina, Dónal, and Maya, the lights of my life who make it all matter.